BORDER GAMES

WILLIAM SAVERY

abbott press®
A DIVISION OF WRITER'S DIGEST

Abbott Press books may be ordered through booksellers or by contacting:

Abbott Press
1663 Liberty Drive
Bloomington, IN 47403
www.abbottpress.com
Phone: 1-866-697-5310

ISBN: 978-1-4582-0950-4 (sc)
ISBN: 978-1-4582-0949-8 (e)

Library of Congress Control Number: 2013908838

Printed in the United States of America.

Abbott Press rev. date: 05/21/2013

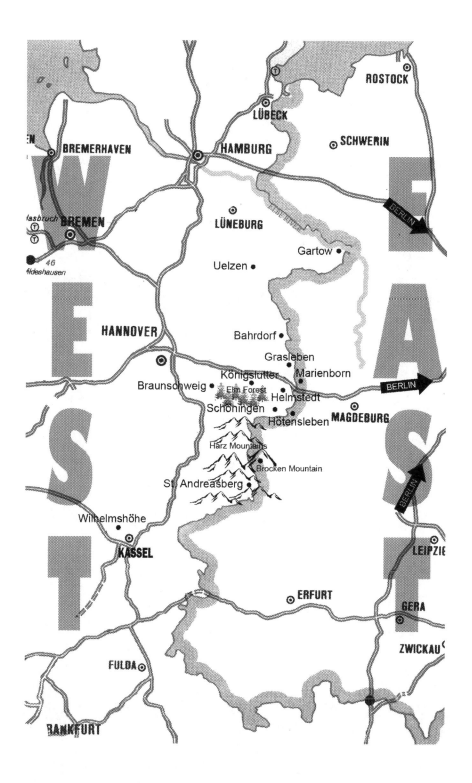

I

The summer breeze carried the sweet smell of chestnuts up from the valley below. The afternoon sun shone brightly and glistened through the fluttering leaves and the young soldier temporarily got lost in memories of his morning journey.

He was awakened by someone calling: "Fall in; fall in." He snapped out of his dreaming just as the other five soldiers were throwing their duffle bags in a heap and were already lining up in a row. "On the double, private," came the words as he too piled his duffle bag and hurried to his position at the end of the line.

"Welcome to Wilhelmshöhe and the 318th. This will be your home for the next several months. We hope you had a good train trip up from Frankfurt."

The private thought back again on this morning's trip, his first train ride in his entire life. He had found the last seat in a second-class nonsmoking compartment while the other five American soldiers had decided to remain together in the corridor of the express train from Frankfurt. He had taken part in a conversation with three German passengers about the pretty landscape, the weather and the train ride. He had been impressed by their openness and friendliness. From this trip alone he had already decided that he liked this place and the things and people he saw. At the station in Kassel they had waited for 30 minutes for the military bus to pick them up for the short trip up to Wilhelmshöhe. He had not stayed with the others but had wandered through the train station where everything seemed so strange, new, and exciting. He observed people rushing to get a connection, buying newspapers or getting a bite to eat. It seemed that he blended into the crowd. Even with his uniform on, his monkey suit as he affectionately called it, no one even seemed to notice him. And now here they were at their new duty station and he was looking forward with great excitement and apprehension.

"Now that I finally have your complete attention," he continued, looking at the short line of soldiers, "I am Corporal Smith, your barracks coordinator. If you have a problem in the barracks you see me and only me. After role call you will each be assigned a room with a roommate who is now working his shift. You will go to the dispensary and get bedding and towels to take to your rooms. After that you will have two hours free time so that you can get acclimated to your new surroundings, set up your living space and to rest up from your long journey. I understand that most of you probably got very little sleep in the last 36 hours. Dinner is in the mess hall is at 1800 hours. Any questions?"

"Good, when I call your name, respond with "Here, sir." He began: "Gehrling?"

"Here, sir," responded the second soldier in the line.

"Cummings?"

"Here, sir."

"Curtin?"

"Here, sir."

"Savery?"

"Here, sir."

"Tow . . . ?" broke off the corporal, who suddenly got a strange, surprised expression on his face.

"Savery?" repeated the corporal again, "Are you a 988?"

"Point 3" responded the private half in a boasting sort of way.

"Everyone except Savery, fall out. My assistant Private Scott here will accompany you into the barracks." With that the corporal turned to a lieutenant standing nearby, and the two of them spoke quietly for a few moments. Private first class Savery was still standing at attention. He wondered what the discussion was about. It seemed to have something to do with his MOS. 988. But didn't everyone have basically the same MOS? Wasn't everyone a linguist? Suddenly the Pfc. felt the two of them staring at him.

"Savery, where have you been? We've been waiting for you. Follow me!"

"But, sir, my duffle bag."

"Just leave it; someone will take care of it. They're waiting for you in the Ice House. We've got to go now!" And with that Corporal Smith approached the lieutenant again, said a few words, saluted and started walking away with a "Come on, on the double, Private!"

The private just followed as fast as he could, wondering where he was going and what was waiting for him. They left the barracks area, which was surrounded by hundreds of trees. For the first time the private realized how big the area was. The many buildings looked like old college dormitories with accompanying structures for vehicles, laundry, heat and supply. As they hurried along, they emerged onto an open plain well over a half mile long and several hundred feet wide, which was lined with oak and maple trees. Along this open field were immense metal towers dwarfing the trees. Savery noticed that from the top of these towers every five were wired together forming a rhombic pattern set up in random groups and seemingly aimed in random directions. Through a break in the trees a ruin of what appeared to be a bombed out castle could be seen a couple miles away.

"What kind of a place is this?" the private asked.

"It used to be a camouflaged Nazi air field" responded Smith, "Not one single bomb fell on it. From the air it looked like a farm but during the war there were dozens of planes here with hundreds of pilots and other soldiers. It was not discovered until our troops actually entered it near the end of the war. That's why it's in such good condition today and that's why we still use it but for drastically different reasons. The two of them walked in silence for five minutes. Suddenly the sound of two approaching airplanes burst over them. The swusch of the engines was sudden and piercing and Pfc. Savery twisted around to try to see the source of the sound. Corporal Smith hardly reacted at all but rather laughed and shouted: "Wave, they're taking our picture."

"Who's taking our picture? Who is it?"

"They're MiG 17's. They want to know where our antennas are aimed. The Warsaw Pact maneuvers are going on right now just a few miles from here in East Germany," added Smith.

"The Warsaw Pact . . . Just a few miles from here?" Savery had of course heard of the Warsaw Pact in his endless training lectures in security school back in Virginia. It was a military alliance led by the Soviets, which encompassed military support from the Eastern European countries under Soviet domination. It was created in the early 50's to defend against NATO, the North Atlantic Treaty Organization, essentially run by the US and created to defend Western Europe against the Soviets. All of this resulted in a divided Germany with a five-kilometer demilitarized border zone penned by Churchill as the Iron Curtin and the recent construction of the Berlin Wall, which Savery had only heard about. But this was still just a game and seldom taken seriously by soldiers learning to be linguists, who would soon be part of the early warning system to prevent a Soviet sneak attack and Savery remembered how non-seriously he had taken these lectures. And now Warsaw Pact maneuvers were going on just a few miles from here? Were we so close to East Germany?

"Don't worry, we're right behind them. We'll chase them back over the border." And with that two F17's roared over the air field, barely 30 seconds behind the MiG's. Once again the piercing sound of fighter jet engines shattered the afternoon tranquility. "This happens every day during their maneuvers; they do it to us and we do it to them. It's all part of the game."

They continued their walk in silence a couple more minutes when on the left in the trees appeared a building which looked like a control tower rising just above tree top level. It was encircled by a 20-foot-high barbed-wire fence. Behind the fence guard dogs were lying watching us. As we drew closer the dogs began to bark.

"The Ice House," said Pfc. Smith to Savery as a heavily armed MP appeared at the gate. "I have Savery with me; inform them inside." Several minutes went by before word came back to escort him in. The two of them entered the building and were taken to a small room near the entrance. An army captain came into the room and dismissed the Corporal, who saluted and left. The Pfc. saluted the captain and said: "Pfc. Savery reporting, sir."

"Captain Baer, commanding officer of the 318th. We'll get security to check your papers, fingerprint you, check you in and get you proper identification. I see you already have top secret code word clearance. That's very good because we are very busy and we need you now; we've been waiting for you."

The check-in process took about forty five minutes, during which time the Pfc. did not leave this small room. He could hear people scurrying around, and what he thought was the sound of teletypes and he longed to be part of the process.

Finally he was presented a laminated ID card with his picture on it and the words Top Secret Code Word stamped at an angle. He was to pick this up upon entering this building, to wear it every second he was on duty and surrender it upon leaving. He was never to take this off premises. Just as he was hanging the ID card around his neck, Captain Baer entered the room. "Good, all set then. Let's take a tour of the building," he said as he led Savery through a set of heavy steel double doors. On the other side of the doors was a whirlwind of activity. Soldiers in fatigues and men in civilian clothing were racing about. At least fifty persons were engaged in looking at screens, having small group discussions, comparing notes, all seemingly engaged in urgent business. There were eight to ten offices where persons were entering and exiting.

Further in they entered a huge room, in the center of which was a circle of approximately 30 teletype machines and inside the circle going from one teletype to the next was a man in civilian clothing. At each teletype he would read the last several pages of print with amazing speed and then would break the last printed page and let the printed paper fall outside the circle before continuing to the next.

"That's Burt Nelson. Works for NSA; he's a GS 19, best there is. If it's happening in the East he practically knows it before they do. Knows ten languages fluently. He's checking transcripts coming in live from our satellite stations along the border, trying to break their code. He'll do it too; it's just a matter of time." They watched him for a few moments and then went on. Around the edges of this massive room other teletypes were also whirring, spitting out reams of paper full of intelligence. Captain Baer explained that the teletypes in the center were printing intelligence processed and sent electronically by their best linguists at the satellite stations. If these linguists could identify the radio activity as being from or to a high ranking officer, they would try to transcribe it as close to live time as possible and send it on to headquarters, whereas the teletypes on the edges were printing intelligence from hours or even days before. So all conversations were recorded on six inch tapes, then the seemingly most important were immediately transcribed and sent on, then the remaining conversations were picked up daily by couriers and brought to headquarters, where they were processed hours or even days after they actually occurred live. During the Warsaw Pact maneuvers there was so much radio activity that even thousands of conversations had to be brought to headquarters to be transcribed.

As the tour continued, Savery slowly got the complete picture. There were thousands of different military units in the Warsaw Pact, ranging from dozens of generals from the various armies down through every type of unit, including artillery, missile units, nuclear missile units, infantry, motorized infantry, armored, radar, motor pool, mess hall, supply, laundry and so on for endless units. Even every platoon had a call sign. Each of these communicated with each other by radio. A general naturally would not identify himself as a general, for security reasons he would want to keep that secret, but would have a call sign, a normal, everyday word, assigned to his unit that would make him sound like even the smallest most unimportant unit that existed, perhaps an infantry squad, and the goal was to make each and every unit unidentifiable.

Once a year the Warsaw Pact would go on maneuvers for three weeks and at one exact predetermined minute with every unit physically moving around, all thousand plus units would change their call signs to some other call sign and at the exact same time change the frequency they transmitted on the radio dial. This would lead to confusion on the part of NATO intelligence. In one way or another, this affected their ability to gather intelligence from fighter plane traffic to radar to Morse code, to low level, to high level, to grass. A big deal!

Captain Baer explained that this year's maneuvers had been going on for two weeks already and seemed to be occurring just over the border from the 318th, making it the main source of intelligence gathering.

"Let's go on to the transcription rooms," said Captain Baer as they rounded a corner and started down a long hallway, "These soldiers are the life blood of our mission. Through schooling and experience on the job they have attained the highest level of proficiency in their language and we count on them to do the impossible." Entering the first room on the left Savery could see three soldiers sitting at typewriters; each had a set of earphones on and was making his tape rewind to play passages over and over, while all the time typing what he was hearing. "These are our Polish .3's," said the captain, "all trained in Monterey just like you but each of them has also been on the job now for at least a year so they are all very good." The captain stopped and talked with the soldiers and then continued on to more rooms. There were separate rooms for Czech, Hungarian, German and finally Russian. "This is where you'll be working," said Captain Baer entering the room. There were four soldiers, who seemed to be doing exactly the same thing as the first three but with the Russian language." These are the only 988.3's we have here at the moment. The others are all out at border cites. So you have arrived at a very opportune time for us with the Warsaw Pact maneuvers going on."

"But, if they're .3's, how can I be a .3? I haven't worked a single minute on the job much less an entire year."

"It's simple, each of these soldiers had one full year of Russian at Monterey and then came here, where they worked their way up and drastically improved their understanding of the Russian language. In fact we're hoping that they re-up and stay here on the job. We need them. But you, you had 48 weeks but then volunteered to take another 27 weeks. You are a member of the first ever Monterey R-75 class and the Army is hoping that you'll be very successful and your experimental program in language school will become the norm."

Pfc. Savery thought back to his Monterey Russian class. Seventy one soldiers had started the class but by week 48 only twenty two had graduated and then the best 7 were asked if they wanted to continue on for another twenty seven weeks. For that each had to extend his enlistment for one additional year. Of the seven only two were sent to Germany, Jones to the south in Bavaria and Savery here in the north. The other five including one NSA employee and one Navy captain had never said where they were being assigned and even Doyle disappeared off the map.

Pfc. Savery's mind wandered all the way back more than two years to his basic training in 1963 and how he had become a Russian linguist. He had enlisted in the Army rather than being drafted because he thought he would get a better military occupation specialty or MOS. During the fourth week of basic his platoon had gone on an overnight march. Exhausted and without any sleep they arrived back to their barracks at 7 a.m. But instead of getting dismissed to sleep, the entire platoon was marched to a testing center where they took a 57-question exam in a made-up language to measure their ability to learn a foreign language. After the timed, hour-long test they were marched to breakfast and then the training day just continued without sleep. The private had totally forgotten about the test, when a week later the results were shared with the troops. Most had done very poorly and were thus eliminated from foreign language study. Most of these received orders to join the infantry or artillery. A few had answered between 15 and 25 questions correctly. These soldiers received orders to learn Vietnamese. Savery realized that most everyone was being assigned to the building war zone in Vietnam and he hoped that he would not be.

Only a very few received a grade above 25. Savery received a score of 53 correct answers, nearly perfect. In a conversation with some placement officers, he was offered the opportunity to pick his own language to study from Russian, Chinese Mandarin, or Arabic. He picked Russian, thinking it would provide the widest range of future possibilities and with Russian he would most probably be assigned to Alaska, Turkey, or West Germany. After Basic training he was assigned to the Defense Language Institute in Monterey, California to study the Russian language. The school, which offered more than thirty languages, was said to be the best language school on the planet.

"Sergeant Kraft here will get you started and show you the ropes," said Captain Baer as he gained Kraft's attention, who took off his earphones and stood up. Just as the captain was about to leave the room, Burt Nelson entered the room, introduced himself simply as Nelson and after greeting Savery, he tried to catch him up on the immediate situation.

"We've been trying for almost two weeks to identify every single unit in the maneuvers. We are almost there," Nelson began. "Once we can identify one more unit, it will all fall into place for another year. For this past year the commanding general of the Warsaw Pact, Five Star Soviet General Grozniy, has been identifying himself on the radio simply as "dacha," we think he now identifies himself as "beryoza" but we have been unable to confirm this and unfortunately the only way to confirm it is if he makes a mistake. We're all searching for that one big mistake. Pay attention to Kraft, he knows what he's doing!" and with that Nelson and Captain Baer returned to the teletype room.

Kraft was very helpful; he explained how to use the typewriter, how to load the special three layer paper, how to mount the six-inch tape onto the tape recorder/player and how to use the foot pedal. He let Savery sit down at his machine and listen to what he had been listening to; he showed him what he had just typed and how it was identical to what was on the tape. After about ten brief minutes, Kraft said: "Time for you to actually do it on your own typewriter. Here, take this station." Savery sat down and for the very first time he realized that the typewriter had the Cyrillic alphabet. It was a Russian typewriter! He had never been taught how to type much less to type in Russian. After the Pfc. explained this, Kraft told Savery to play with the typewriter for a few minutes that he would get used to it.

After a couple minutes Kraft led Savery to a corner of the room. "Take a tape, any one you want." Savery stared at the mountain of six-inch tape boxes; there had to be several hundred making the peak of the pile of boxes at least five feet high.

"Do we have to transcribe all these?" he said as he jokingly covered his eyes with one hand while sticking his other hand deeply into the pile and pulling one random tape out with the other.

"You'll get used to it in a hurry. Soon it will be second nature to you. Let's take it back to your station and we'll get started." Kraft helped put the tape on the recorder/player and the paper into the typewriter and helped Savery punch in the identifying code with the date and the transcriber's initials: 06/09/BS. "OK, you're on your own, no more explanations." With that the sergeant returned to his own station, put on his ear phones, pressed his foot pedal to start the player and started to type.

Smith was right, after a few moments the Pfc. felt right at home. He listened to the first conversation; it was in really simple Russian and seemed to just be a check of their radio connection. It was only two minutes long, just five short lines. Even then it took Savery fifteen minutes to type it.

He pressed the foot pedal to hear the next conversation.

"Luna, luna, ya beryoza. Priyom." No one responded. After about fifteen seconds he repeated: "Luna, luna, ya beryoza. Priyom." No one responded again. A third time the caller continued: "Luna, luna, ya dacha . . . uh, uh ya beryoza. Priyom," Luna responded and after establishing radio contact, they simply both signed off. Savery just sat there. Could it be this easy, had he heard correctly, was this what everyone was searching for? Savery listened to the exchange a dozen times. There was no doubt about it, he had heard it correctly.

The Pfc. stood up and walked into the teletype room and stopped near the closest teletype. There was Burt Nelson inside the ring going from teletype to teletype. As he was reaching the location where Savery was standing, Savery said apologetically and almost afraid: "Uh, sir, I think I found it." Nelson just ignored him and read his way around the entire circle. As he approached again, Savery repeated: "Sir, I think I found it."

Suddenly Nelson stopped, stared at Savery and then rushed off to the Russian transcription room, the Pfc. following behind. In the room he sat down at Savery's station, put on the head phones, pressed the foot pedal, listened to the exchange, and then listened to the exchange again.

"I'll be damned!" he exclaimed as he stood up and exited the room.

II

A week had passed. Seven long very busy days. The Warsaw Pact maneuvers had ended, their soldiers had returned to their normal barracks, and the mountain of unprocessed Russian tapes had disappeared. Seven days since Savery saw his first MiG. Seven days since the Warsaw Pact code had been broken. Only six days since Private first class Savery had been promoted to Specialist fifth class Savery. SPC-5, E-5, Sergeant Savery—it had a ring about it.

But Savery had little time to celebrate his promotion and in fact was not really impressed with his would-be success. He had broken the code by pure coincidence and realized that there were many .3's here who were far better than he. He had learned how to type in Russian very quickly and had helped transcribe the mountain of tapes "in record time," as Captain Baer put it. Since then it seemed like time was flying past. He had to send all his fatigues and his two dress uniforms to the company laundry to have new insignias sewed on, on one shoulder lightning bolts, the symbol of Military Intelligence. Of course on each sleeve his new SPC-5 chevron.

As he sat back and relaxed in the cab of the five ton communications truck, he thought back on the last seven days. That first night he had volunteered to work until midnight transcribing, even though Captain Baer and several others had told him to quit for the night and go to the barracks. Only after the midnight shift had arrived did he agree to accept a jeep ride back across the air strip.

After the jeep had dumped him in the center of the dorms and had driven off, Savery suddenly realized that he didn't know what dorm he was supposed to sleep in or in what room or where his bedding was or even where his duffle bag was. Fortunately, he entered the correct dorm where he asked the night duty for Corporal Smith, who soon came out to the night duty station. Seeing the Pfc. he said: "Are you just now coming from the Ice House? I brought you there ten hours ago!"

"It got a little hectic, they needed some help; I did what I could."

Realizing that the Pfc. was probably exhausted, Corporal Smith grabbed a pile of bedding, escorted Savery to an empty room on the main floor, told him to crash for the night and then see him at 0800. Within five minutes Savery was sound asleep.

Since that first night he had oriented himself with the entire base including the dorm area, the mess hall, the barber shop, the PX and the medical section and been given a routine medical exam but which also featured a hearing test. "You're going to enter this sound proof chamber, sit down, put on the earphones and hold this devise in your hands. When I give you the signal through the window, I will start the test. When you hear a sound you will simply press the button on your device and when the sound stops you simply let up off the button and wait for the next sound. Some sounds will last longer than other sounds, some will be high pitched, some low, some in your left ear some in your right, some in both. We just want to check your range of hearing. While the test is going on, the program out here will print a graph of your reaction time to each sound in milliseconds and then print out a very specific score. When the test ends, I'll open the door. Are there any questions?" Savery just shook his head. Savery entered the chamber, put on the earphones, picked up the device and the hearing test started. After a few sounds, Savery closed his eyes so that he could better concentrate on the sounds. Suddenly the door opened and the technician said: "Test over, Golden Ears, thank you very much." He had apparently done well.

Last night he actually got to go off base. Ever since he had heard about the Friday night military bus provided to the center of Wilhelmshöhe, he had been looking forward to it and as Friday approached he discovered that many soldiers would be going. It was great to wear civilian clothing for the first time. They were left off at a string of bars after being reminded to stick together and to be at this exact spot at 2400 hours for the mile long return trip back up the hill.

Two soldiers said they would look after Savery. Corporals Cromby and Rolland had been great friends since their Russian language school days at Monterey and after their basic 48-week course, they had both gone to security school in Virginia in the same class and somehow, miraculously, both been sent to the 318th. In two months they were scheduled to be discharged and sent home, one to West Virginia and one to Vermont. After exiting the bus, Cromby said: "Well, where will we begin, the STERN as usual?"

"Great idea! I hope Lotte and Andrea are there." Savery noticed how Roland pronounced their names with a German accent.

"Are they German girls? You know real German girls?" Savery asked.

"We know dozens. Every Friday night the Stern is full of German girls; we just happen to really like Lotte and Andrea; they're really cute and they like US soldiers; they like us. That's why they're always here. Maybe they'll find someone to marry them and take them to America."

"Do you want to marry one of them?" asked Savery.

"Hell no, but we get along great with them just the same," said Roland.

The Stern was chuck-full of young people. Basically it was half US soldiers from the 318th and half local German girls in their late teens or very early twenties. Almost every girl was pretty, casually but attractively dressed and all were very out-going and friendly. Lotte and Andrea were there waiting for Roland and Cromby and they sat down with them. Savery was introduced to each and each reached out her hand to shake hands with him. "Sehr angenehm," said one of them. He had no idea what it meant. As time went on and after a couple beers both Cromby and Roland lapsed into German for the rest of the night. Savery had no idea they spoke German. He thought they were Russian linguists. He gradually noticed that every soldier, several of whom he recognized as Russian linguists, was speaking to some degree in German and he thought that he should be too. It looked like they were having fun. He asked Roland where he learned to speak German and he said right here in the Stern.

"Buy yourself a German dictionary; keep it with you always when you're off base. Then use it and have some fun!" This morning, before coming to the motor pool, he had gone to the PX and bought a Langenscheidt's pocket English/German dictionary. He put it in his fatigues pocket. It cost 85 cents. Savery promised himself to try to meet more and more Germans.

Just as he was fishing around in his pocket to get the dictionary, someone called: "OK, Sergeant, break's over. Time to take your driving test." Staff Sergeant Pereau was an 18-year veteran of the motor pool, who had seen action in Korea and because of that he mistrusted people. He preferred the company of engines, machines and tools. Staff Sergeant Pereau's hands were always greasy and he smelled of fluids and gasoline. He was a legend in the 318th. He could fix any machine. Sergeant Savery had been warned not to cross Staff Sergeant Pereau but for some reason the two of them struck it off and seemed to function as best friends.

"It's been a pleasure riding with you these last two days teaching you the inner secrets of the jeep, the three ton troop carrier, and the five ton communications truck. All we have left is to test you on this five-ton communications truck and then you'll be able to drive everything we have except for tow trucks, trailer trucks, and tanks."

"Do we really have tanks?" asked Savery.

"Not directly, but they're close by," responded the staff sergeant. He continued: "Now follow my directions precisely as we go along. We will drive around the grounds here, then, when I think you're ready, go out onto the Kreisstrasse and then onto the Landesstrasse and then onto a Bundesstrasse and then for two or three exits out onto the Autobahn. We'll see if you're ready for the big time. You know, there's no speed limit here so caution is the key? You're driving a massive truck and we can only hope I've trained you well. OK, start the engine."

He did train the sergeant well and the sergeant passed the road test. Savery couldn't wait to be on his own on the Autobahn with such a big rig.

As it turned out he did not have to wait long.

At 0700 in the mess hall the next morning Sergeant Savery got a message to report to Captain Baer's office in the Ice House at 0930 hours. This was the first time that he had been summoned to the CO's office and Savery had no idea what was going on and so decided to report twenty minutes early. Slowly the captain's waiting room filled up with approximately a dozen soldiers, only some of whom he knew. He recognized one German linguist, a private from electronic maintenance and a soldier from the motor pool. The rest he had no idea who they were; he had never seen the lieutenant before and he wondered how all these soldiers got in without displaying an identity badge like the one he had on.

At precisely 0930, the office door opened and Captain Baer told everyone to come in. He then greeted everyone and said he had handpicked them for a special mission. The soldiers stared at each other and wondered what he was talking about. "I feel that I know each of you well and that each of you has excelled in your own specific area. All of you except for one have been here for over a year." Savery wondered where this was headed as he glanced around at the strange faces. The captain had every one enter the conference

16

room where a huge map of the 318$^{th'}$ was being projected onto the wall. It was the first time the sergeant had seen a map of where the satellite sites were situated. Some were very close by and some seemed very far away. There was a flag near each town where an outpost was situated. There were flags near St. Andreasberg, Schöningen, Bahrdorf and a couple others. For the first time he saw the East/ West German border in great detail as it snaked its way across the map, how it crossed a low plain east of Fulda and zigzagged its way up through the Harz Mountain area to the north and eventually on past Helmstedt, the beginning point of the middle Berlin Corridor. He noticed that all the satellites were very close to the border. And for the first time he saw names of towns in East Germany that he had heard while transcribing tapes-towns like Tanne, Elend, Schirke, Walbeck, Ohrsleben—all just dots on the map within 5 kilometers of the border. Many of them had flags too, probably denoting Soviet units. All so close! This was exciting!

He was still soaking in the map when the captain began: "The Warsaw Pact maneuvers have ended and, so you'll know, the brass was really impressed by the 318th this year. So impressed, in fact, that we've been invited to the NATO exercises, which start next week in Bad Kreuznach near Frankfurt. This will be the first time we'll be represented. More specifically, YOU will represent the military intelligence community."

As he hesitated a murmur arose in the room. "I will lead the convoy and all fifteen of you will be going, probably actually driving. We'll be taking four jeeps, a troop carrier, a tow truck and two communication trucks. We'll join the main convoy north of Frankfurt in Giessen. Our goal is to show the brass that they too make vital intelligence mistakes on the radio. Half of you will work with the Green Army and half with the Blue Army." The meeting continued with a lively question and answer period. They eventually watched training films about NATO exercises, about security and about living for days in the forest.

The drive to Bad Kreuznach was every bit as exciting as the sergeant had hoped. He felt so powerful and free as his communications truck raced toward the meeting point near Giessen. He had never seen so many military vehicles in his life, there must be three hundred vehicles right here, he thought as the convoy entered this pre-staging area north of Frankfurt. Captain Baer had jumped out of his jeep and was directing traffic: "To the left, I said!" he shouted to the driver of our troop carrier. Eventually the captain managed to get all their vehicles together and they all went to the outdoor mess area. The food was good and Savery was unaware exactly how hungry he was. After lunch the captain conducted a brief five minute meeting, reminding everyone to stay in line and follow him all the way to where they would exit off the Autobahn. Just five kilometers from the exit was the final staging area near the little town of Planig. They would meet there one more, final time before they split up. An hour and a half later the 318th was together again just outside Planig. Ten minutes after all vehicles arrived, Captain Baer presented a Lieutenant Carlson. "Lieutenant Carlson has been assigned to the Blue Army. Half of you will be under his command and therefore be part of the Blue Army the other half will be under my command in the Green Army. As you know, your task is to monitor radio transmissions of the opposing army and report any security breaches to your commanding generals. Are there any questions?"

"Yes, sir, I have a question!"

"Go ahead, Sergeant D'Amico; ask your question."

"Well, sir, it's taken months and perhaps even years to correctly identify all the Russian units we know. Only through all our work have we gotten so good at it. But how can we identify any NATO unit. We don't know anything about NATO radio protocol. We don't know their format. We don't know their call signs, or their locations or their frequencies on the radio. It seems to me, we'll be working in a void. The maneuvers will be over long before we even get started."

"Great question," said Captain Baer. "We have an ace in the hole, but more about that later. Any other questions?"

"Yes, sir, I have a question," said Sergeant Braun, "Where is Lieutenant Carlson from? And is he familiar with our mission?"

"The lieutenant works at Headquarters Intelligence Europe in Frankfurt. He's one of those persons I told you were impressed by us. He's here to see you in action," said Captain Baer. A moment of silence followed and for some reason Sergeant Savery hoped he would be assigned to the Green Army.

"Good," said Captain Baer. "The following eight will be assigned to the Blue Army: Lieutenant Carlson, sergeants Baker, Patrick, Eiger, Jefferson, Savery, D'Amico and Corporal Henderson. The rest of you will be with the Green Army." For some reason Savery got a strange feeling in his stomach.

But his ill feelings quickly subsided, Lieutenant Carlson turned out to be a very likeable, pleasant person, who wanted to see the members of the 318th in action. The whole group liked him. The eight soldiers and half the vehicles were escorted to some really little town of approximately 150 residents in the NATO training area, which turned out to be 20 kilometers by 15 kilometers and which encompassed every village located in the area. As a result of this, civilian cars, bikes and even pedestrians were everywhere to be seen and these German civilians seemed really curious about the American military presence. Those soldiers assigned to the Blue Army were convoyed an additional ten kilometers and were halted on the top of a high hill, where the vehicles were parked in random positions.

The rest of the day was spent setting up pup tents and ten larger thirty by thirty foot tents for officer meetings and other maneuver business. Even the latrines and our communications truck were inside tents. In addition one fifty by one hundred foot tent was put up to act as a mess tent for the soldiers in the immediate vicinity. All tents except for pup tents were very unusual. Each was really a tent within a tent so that no light escaped while entering or leaving. This would help keep the location of our units concealed during the nighttime hours. Light travels far at night and any escaping light could lead to disaster. Sergeant Savery noticed that there were tents as far as he could see in every direction.

At 1600 hours Lieutenant Carlson summoned everyone together for a meeting. He explained that they would work in twelve hour shifts and that Patrick, Eiger, and Jefferson would be working the day shift with him from 0800 till 2000, whereas D'Amico, Baker and Savery would be working the nightshift from 2000 to 0800. Corporal Henderson would also be working the night shift to fix any mechanical glitches which might occur with the radio equipment during the night. He suggested that everyone stay in the pup tent area when not working and that everyone get plenty of sleep.

"Now for our ace in the hole, as Captain Baer put it. I have here two copies of a top secret manual specifically produced for us for these exercises. The brass realizes that there's no way for us to even begin to gather any real intelligence without having a starting point. So they came up with this manual identifying every single unit in the exercises from the highest officers to the most seemingly insignificant platoons. Essentially we have "broken" the NATO code just as you broke the Warsaw Pact code. We've done the work for you! All you have to do is listen in to any units you want; you'll already know which ones they are, and listen for security breaches. The 318th's group in the Green Army has the same manual so you're basically in a game with them so see who can find the most breaches."

The sergeants gathered around the manual, trying to get a good view of it. The first fifty pages were on green paper, the next fifty on blue paper. Across the top of the page were column headings from left to right: unit, unit commander, connected to, call sign, frequency on dial, comments and on the very first line was: Headquarters Green Army, Gen. G. Packard; Headquarters Europe, Forest. 0930 megahertz. There he was, commanding general of the Green Army with all conceivable information to identify him. The first two pages each contained the same information about twenty five officers in the Green Army. The manual proceeded through hundreds of units in descending order of importance.

"Oh, there's just one more thing. Unlike back in the 318th, these vehicles have radios, with which you can call out, but don't do this. Only Corporal Henderson has been properly trained and only he has been licensed to operate these radios. Is that clear?"

"Yes, sir," answered every soldier.

"The training exercises begin tonight at 2000. At that time D'Amico, Savery, Henderson and Baker will be on duty in the communications truck. Good luck, men." ended the lieutenant.

At 2000 hours the four soldiers were at their station, ready to gather more intelligence than their fellow soldiers in the Green Army. Their radios were on and they were searching the frequencies for traffic. But the exercises started very slowly and for the first three hours they intercepted only a few dozen very normal transmissions mostly from low ranking units and half of what they heard was from their own army. It seemed that the US forces were just as careful as the Soviets. Around 1130 the three got into a conversation about food.

"When is supper being served?" asked Archer. "I'm hungry already."

"I think from midnight to 1 a.m.," said Baker.

"I don't think we can all go together to the mess tent," said Savery. "Someone has to stay on duty here and man the receivers."

"We can leave Henderson here and we'll all three go together,' added Archer.

"Where IS Henderson? I haven't seen him in a half hour?" asked Savery.

"He discovered a problem with one of the receivers and he's taken it somewhere for repair," said Baker.

"I hope he gets back soon; I'm hungry," repeated Baker. "What's our code word tonight anyway?"

No one knew the code word and they had to look it up on the daily parameters sheet. It was "Lion." Why it was Lion, one could only guess but the idea was to memorize the daily code word and if challenged while walking through the forest from one area to another, one would respond with the code word and allowed to continue on. If one didn't respond with the proper code word he would be taken prisoner and be eliminated from the exercises. It was important to know the code word.

"It's Lion," said Baker. "Remember it now!"

Henderson eventually came back and agreed to man the receivers while the three sergeants went to eat together. Supper was fried chicken, mashed potations, rolls and peas. It tasted good. The way home was totally dark and the soldiers found the total silence unusual. The rest of the night passed without incidence. They heard no breaches of security.

At 2000 hours the next night they reported to the communications truck for their shift. The day crew told them that it had been a slow day and that nothing seemed to be happening. And so it continued for about a week. The most noteworthy events turned out not to be the listening process but the off duty process. Being confined generally to the pup tent and mess tent areas, heating water in helmets to shave and wash, hanging around, all seemed fun for a while but the novelty soon wore off. Lieutenant Carlson said to cope with it, enjoy the challenge and everything would work out.

As time went on, the night shift crew noticed the quirks of the individual radio operators and played games with each other; identifying units by the way they used their radio transmitters even before they began their conversations. One radio operator would press his transmitter button, then let up, then press his button again before he would actually speak. And he did this every time. Another pressed his button to send but waited a full five seconds to begin. Still another would begin with the utterance "uhh." The crew decided to listen to twelve basic units and ignore all the rest; they jumped from one of their frequencies to the next and everything became simpler and simpler. Still they noticed no intelligence breaches.

At 0300 one night Baker came up with a strange idea. "Let's mimic them. Let's pretend to be them."

"Are you serious?" said D'Amico. "We can't do that. The lieutenant warned us."

"But it's just a game!" said Baker and he grabbed the transmitter microphone. Before another word could be said, Baker was pressing the send button on the frequency assigned to one of the generals. He held the button for a few seconds and then released it. He pressed the button again, held it for a few seconds and released it again.

"What are you doing?" said Savery, "Are you crazy?"

But it was too late. The general answered, "This is Harvest; who's calling?"

The three soldiers started at each other as the general repeated. "This is Harvest; who's calling? Identify yourself."

"My God!" said Savery. "Can they identify us?"

Baker dropped the transmitter microphone. He had not expected anyone to answer. He was just having some fun. A big argument followed between the three and it was decided not to do this again. They agreed to never mention this to anyone, even Corporal Henderson. No one could ever know what they had done.

The following night was overcast and very dark, so dark that Baker got slightly separated from the other two as they walked back to their communications truck from supper. "Where are you guys?" he said out loud in the darkness.

Suddenly an almost whispering voice out of the darkness said. "Quiet down, what's the code word?"

Baker was shocked and surprised that someone was so close to him and he had no idea what the code word was. "What's the code word?" he too asked totally out loud, hoping that the sergeants could hear him. But no one answered.

The voice next to him said, "Bang, you're dead!"

"Bang, I'm dead!" laughed Baker out loud. "Hey guys, I'm dead!" With that he rushed off through the trees looking for the communications truck.

As bad as this was, something far worse occurred two nights later. There was so little radio traffic that the three sergeants decided not to monitor their upper level units but started checking out the smaller, less important units just to do something different and much to their surprise many companies, platoons, and even squads were very active, some making radio contact every five minutes. This seemed strange but still there was nothing of importance to be heard. At 0030 hours in the mess tent there was no mention of anything strange going on.

Returning from supper, fried chicken again, the same lower level units were still very active and seemed to be louder, meaning that they must be closer. Baker sent Henderson over to headquarters to tell them. After Henderson left, Savery decided to go out to the jeep and listen in from the jeep radio thus doubling their listening capabilities and during the next thirty minutes Baker continually went back and forth from the communications truck to the jeep to coordinate efforts. Finally something was happening! Baker thought he heard distant popping as if coming from blank M1 rounds. But at the same time there was no unusual radio traffic from the higher units. Strange! Suddenly Savery heard totally five by five: "Mail, Mail, this is Fire, over" and an answer: "Fire, Fire, this is Mail, over." These guys are close, Savery thought, very close. "Mail, Mail, execute the plan, over."

"Executing, the plan now," came the answer.

Suddenly there were shapes moving around in the darkness within a few meters from the jeep and there was a pop and sssssss of a teargas canister. "I'm being gassed, gulped Savery as he frantically searched the floor of the jeep for his gas mask. He struggled but got the mask on just as he felt someone trying to turn the door handle from the outside. He braced the handle shut with his shoulder and

24

reached across the jeep to hold the other door shut. He was gagging and his lungs burned but he dared not move. At the same time he became aware of shouting and yelling from the communications truck; they were getting it too! Suddenly, as quickly as it all began, it ended. From the opposite direction foot soldiers from the Blue Army showed up and drove the attacking Green soldiers off, taking several prisoners. An officer told us everything was OK and to just continue on with our activities.

Thirty minutes later, Baker, D'Amico and Savery were still gagging and choking from the tear gas and as they sat in the communications truck they hatched a plan to get even. They decided to actually call some units to see what would happen. Baker started; after all, it was his original idea.

He set the radio to an unassigned frequency and called a Green Army missile battery "Roof, Roof, this is Door, over." He repeated it again after a few seconds. There was no unit in the exercise on either side, which identified itself as "Door," Roof answered: "This is Roof, please identify yourself." Of course, Baker did not identify himself and they all thought that this was fun, better than being gassed. They made about six additional calls but decided it wasn't exciting enough because no one knew who was calling.

They changed the idea. Baker chose a midlevel officer in artillery and called him and identified himself as an artillery unit from the other army. "Light, Light, this is River. Request permission to enter your net, over." Light answered but hesitated and said, "Wait one!" After a couple calls it was decided to go up the ladder. They checked the call signs and chose the second in command of the Green Army, Eagle, and the second in command of the Blue Army, Hawk. Baker pressed the microphone and said: "Eagle, Eagle, this is Hawk. Request permission to enter your net." Eagle, who clearly knew that Hawk should not know this call sign and should not be calling him, answered, "Wait one!" A moment later Eagle called back: "Hawk, Hawk, this is Eagle. Authenticate Hotel India, over."

Sergeant Baker had no idea what Eagle was talking about and did not respond. This was something new that none of the three had ever heard. They quickly chose another high ranking officer, this time from the Blue Army and did the same thing. "Bicycle, Bicycle, this is Farm. Request permission to enter your net, over." "Wait one," came the response and then after a couple minutes, "Authenticate Charlie Echo." They made about ten attempts to make contact between the armies, including generals of one army calling platoons in the other. Finally they decided to end their game before they were caught. "Teargas us, will you!" said Baker.

A funny thing happened, as time went on, chaos started on the radio. No one wanted to talk with anyone; everyone wanted the caller to authenticate letters and it finally got to the point where, when one unit said something like: "Authenticate Alpha Zebra," the other one would answer: "No, YOU authenticate Alpha Zebra."

At 0410 generals from both armies broadcast a message to all troops: "Abort, abort!" And with that the NATO exercises came to an abrupt end.

Thirty hours later as the 318th came together again just outside Planig for the return trip to home base, Captain Baer debriefed his troops. Something had gone wrong in the exercises and no one was sure what, how, or why. It was decided to end the exercises before the Soviets learned any more about our communications system, the captain said, they had undoubtedly learned too much already.

III

The following Thursday Captain Baer summoned Sergeant Savery to his office and told him he had a special mission for him. Savery thought back to the last time that expression was used, but this turned out to be totally different.

"I have decided to send you up to our most northern border site for a couple weeks; how does that sound, Sergeant?"

"Which site is that?" asked Savery. "Helmstedt?"

"No, we have no 318th soldiers assigned directly in Helmstedt. Helmstedt is the Autobahn border crossing point through the Iron Curtin, the beginning of the middle Berlin Corridor. Its official name is Check Point Alpha but no one refers to it that way. Because of the huge Soviet presence just across the border, we have assigned more and more of our linguists just north of there in Bahrdorf. It's actually in the British zone."

Savery had heard of Bahrdorf several times but wasn't actually sure where it was. He had never actually met a linguist, who had been assigned there.

The captain continued, "One of our three .3 Russian translators there, Staff Sergeant Krastner, has been granted an emergency leave to go back to the States. Apparently his father is near death back in Ohio. He should be back in about fourteen days."

"Sounds good, sir," answered Savery. "When do I leave?"

"Four hours from now," answered the captain. "We'll put you on the 1425 military train in Kassel; it stops only in Goettingen, Salzgitter and Helmstedt on its way to Berlin. Someone will pick you up in Helmstedt."

Back in his room the sergeant packed his duffle bag with all his military clothing and then his only suitcase with his civilian clothing. He hoped it was OK to even take a suitcase, but he risked it. After he put on his fatigue uniform, he said goodbye to a few friends and went outside to wait for the jeep, which would take him to the train station.

At 1410 hours the military train pulled into the Kassel station on track 5. Sergeant Savery showed his orders to the military conductor and was told to sit anywhere he wanted in the train. He selected a totally empty car and just after the stop in Goettingen he fell asleep. When he woke up, the train was at a full stop. The station sign said "Helmstedt." He was already there. He gathered his belongings and headed out of the station.

Much to his surprise there were many people running into and out of the train station and he had some trouble finding his contact. Finally a Pfc. approached him, identified himself as Private Sanders, grabbed Savery's duffle bag and placed it in the jeep. "Sorry I'm late; it's been a busy day." And with that they were on their way through the center of town.

As they were driving north out of the city, the driver asked if his passenger had ever seen the border crossing. And when he heard that Savery had not, took a sudden sharp right turn onto a very narrow road. After about 300 meters the view opened up onto a huge plaza on the side of the Autobahn just before the actual crossing point. The driver parked the jeep in a space marked "US Military Vehicles Only" and shut off the engine. "Let's go into the restaurant," he said. "We'll get a cup of coffee and look around." Savery had never seen a border crossing before much less such an important one. The Autobahn was narrowed down to one lane headed east into East Germany and about ten cars and six trucks were lined up to go through the

Allied Check Point. The drivers and passengers seemed to be showing passports or identity cards as well as automobile documents. Once a vehicle was cleared to proceed, it continued east through a zigzag pattern to a parking area some four hundred meters down the road at the far end of that parking lot there seemed to be another check point. There seemed to be hundreds of cars lined up for that check point. When Savery asked the driver about the further check point, he was told that the Soviets made it tough for anyone to cross on their way to West Berlin; that their goal was to harass Westerners. "That's already East Germany; that's already Marienborn."

The most imposing feature of the crossing point was not the road but rather the actual border. About half way to the far parking area on each side of the Autobahn there was a twenty meter high guard tower and in them the sergeant could see the outline of soldiers. Before the towers was a ten meter high barbed wire fence which stretched north south across the terrain. On both sides of this fence there seemed to be a hundred meter wide strip of wasteland filled with all sorts of barriers, seemingly designed to keep people out or in and every three hundred meters there was another guard tower. "The death strip!" the driver said matter-of-factly. After about fifteen minutes they continued on their way to Bahrdorf.

The site at Bahrdorf had problems. It was too small; it had old equipment; these were few housing opportunities close by; its main intercept target, the Soviet fifth army had moved 30 kilometers south to Hötensleben across from Schöningen, just far enough away to make radio reception difficult. Plus it was in the British zone. In addition to all this their barracks at Grasleben, an old weapons factory, also housed MP's from the border crossing in Helmstedt and so was always overfull. New transfers were automatically housed in a small, old-fashioned inn or Gasthaus just down the road from the site until room opened up in the weapons factory. Not that troops didn't like the inn, there just wasn't much going on there and Grasleben was just a few minutes from Helmstedt, where there was real night life going on. And the inn had a funny name "Zum weissen Spargel" and when anyone asked what it meant, one had to say "The White Asparagus Inn." Sergeant Savery heard all this from the driver on the way from Helmstedt. "Needless to say, you're staying at the Spargel," the driver laughed.

Just then they took a right hand turn and traveled down a narrow road. After a few hundred meters the site came into view. It indeed looked small and run down, its most predominate feature being the twenty foot high barbed wire fence. The driver did not stop but continued on through some trees. Four hundred meters down the road on the left Savery could see an old farmstead with oddly shaped corrugated fields behind it and on the right across from the farmstead, the actual East-West German border. It was suddenly only 100 meters away from the road which gradually turned to the left and ran parallel to the border. It truly scared Sergeant Savery to be so close to the border.

"Is this safe? Aren't we in the death strip?" he urgently asked the driver.

"In theory, yes," answered the driver," but as long and we don't get any closer, everything will be OK. This is the closest site to the border in the entire six hundred kilometer East-West border. This is the Iron Curtin."

"Is there ever any communication with the other side?" asked Savery.

"Are you kidding, never! East Germans are never allowed close enough to the border to communicate with this side and are too far away for us to hear any cars or machinery. Only their border guards are close enough to hear and they are trained to shoot first. That's their communication!'

"Do Germans ever talk about the other side?"

"Seldom," said the driver. "They hate the Russians."

The driver pulled over and stopped across from the farmstead. Savery realized that they were even closer to the border than they were at the crossing point in Helmstedt. He could actually see the silhouettes of East German or Soviet border guards in a tower that overlooked the immediate area and he realized that these guards were actually looking at the jeep through binoculars. He could see soldiers on foot patrolling the other side of the border, who seemed to be watching them, too. They were so close, that Savery felt he could actually see the expressions on their faces. In the distance he could see a small East German village, which started only a hundred meters east of the death strip. Savery got an uneasy sensation that this place was not safe.

"Are you sure it's safe?" asked the sergeant.

"There's only been one incident here and that happened several years ago when the border had only barbed wire, not guard towers and a death strip."

"That's reassuring," Savery said sarcastically.

"Well, let's go," said the driver, "It's time to get you to your Gasthaus." With that he started the jeep and drove across the narrow road to the farmstead. "We're here; welcome to the Spargel," he said as he shut off the motor. Sure enough the sign read "zum weissen Spargel".

The check in process was more just a dumping off of the bags in an empty room on the second floor, room number 7, locking the room and returning to the jeep.

Minutes later the sergeant was already at the site and was getting an orientation, which was brief because there were only four workrooms. The lieutenant on duty seemed friendly and thorough. He inspected the sergeant's ID with the words "top secret code word," which Captain Baer had given the sergeant before the train trip. The sergeant met several soldiers, mostly Russian and German linguists, only one of whom, a Sergeant Bono, lived at the Spargel. At around 2200 hours Bono was told to take Savery to the Gasthaus in his VW Beetle, to get him properly checked in and to return to the cite at 0800 hours the next day.

There was much activity at the inn when they arrived; the dining room/bar area was full of people and the food smelled delicious. But Savery was exhausted and fell asleep to the sound of laughter and music from below.

For one entire week Sergeant Savery did not leave the immediate area of the site and the Gasthaus except once. He volunteered to work a twelve hour shift every day and the rest of the time he spent at the inn. He slowly became obsessed with the inn and its owners, Horst and Gabriela Schmidt, who turned out to be very friendly toward the sergeant. They were understanding of his meager German language skills, and spoke English and German with him. Savery in turn started using his dictionary again and followed Horst around the inn, sheds and fields, often offering a helpful hand. Gabriela allowed Savery to watch her prepare for the evening dining rush. Gradually they gave glimpses of their past. They were both fourteen-years old at the end of the war. Horst's parents had lived right here on this property, where they ran the Gasthaus. Gabriele lived in the village now immediately across the border less than a kilometer from the inn. Both sets of parents were killed in the same bombing raid. They didn't know which air force had killed their parents but they seemed to have forgiven them. They had then gone through painful years. Horst had reopened the Gasthaus and things got a lot better financially ten years ago, when the US Army opened the site and housed its soldiers in their inn. Three years later Horst and Gabi were married. They were now contemplating a family. Life was good again.

The inn itself was very rustic. It was built in the shape of a three story U. One side contained the living quarters of the owner on the second and third floors and the kitchen space for the inn on the first floor. The middle section contained five rooms for guests on the second floor and five more rooms for guests on the third floor. There seemed to be no central heating but rather a potbellied stove in each room. The left side of the U seemed to contain two small two-room apartments. Connecting all this together in the middle was the entertainment area. This was the heart beat for the inn. It was one very large room. There were about sixteen tables in the center for guests who wanted to eat or just drink and socialize. In one corner a very small space, which appeared to be a space for dancing, on one side of the room a very long bar with twelve bar stools. There was also an electric gambling machine, on which the player inserted a coin and then tried to stop the spinning numbers on a winning combination. The focal point of the entire room was the jukebox. It contained approximately one hundred forty five rpm records. About a quarter of these were old popular songs in English but most were popular German songs.

In the back there were semi-attached quarters for farm animals and farm equipment. Occasionally one could hear and even smell the farm animals. The inn was totally self-sufficient. The farm animals included cows, pigs, chickens, geese, rabbits and goats. From these animals they got milk and eggs as well as fresh meat. There were also two work horses. The fields were full of grass for the animals and wheat for baking at the inn. Having grown up on a dairy farm back in Vermont, Savery was fascinated by the workings of the farm and the inn. There was one thing at the Spargel that Savery had never seen: the spargel. Horst prided himself at producing the area's best asparagus. He had five acres of asparagus fields, which looked like huge corrugated rows of soil. Using a special horse drawn devise, which raised and shaped the soil, Horst created rows of fifteen inches high, very soft soil that were about one foot wide at the top. He then planted thousands of shoots, which he had personally grown from seeds. After they started growing, he covered the endless plants with old newspapers to protect them from the sun. The sun light produced chlorophyll and that turned the asparagus green but the best asparagus was white. For weeks he patrolled and nursed his plants and protected them from the sun until the precise moment when the asparagus became ripe. He then sold all his ripe asparagus to people, who had placed their orders months before. His asparagus industry helped him survive financially and he was very proud of his endeavors.

During the week Savery fell in love with German cooking. There were so many good dishes, most of which he had never heard. There were all kinds of foods with names like Wurst, Schnitzel with the most delicious sauces, Rouladen, Kässler Rippchen, Schweinebraten, Bauernschmaus, Schweinehaxe, Rotkohl, Sauerkraut, Kartoffelsalat, Klöse, and Pommes.

Every evening that he was off duty Savery spent in the dining room in civilian clothes usually with at least one of the other five soldiers staying at the inn. But often he went downstairs alone, sat at the bar, drank German beer on tap and played songs on the juke box. He liked the German songs, called Schlager, especially one entitled "Tausend Mann und ein Befehl." He occasionally got into conversations with young adults who wanted to practice their English or impress their friends. In general the sergeant felt right at home.

Sometime during the week Savery noticed that one thirty-year-old woman was always there and was always drunk. She seemed to be interested in talking with the sergeant but knew no English so they mostly just smiled at each other. As it turned out, her name was Nina and she rented one of the two apartments at the Gasthaus and worked days at the new VW plant in Wolfsburg just twenty kilometers down the road. Horst told Savery not to get involved with her. But one evening she invited him over to her apartment and, not knowing any better, he went with her, probably expecting a closer relationship. She lit some candles and showed him her apartment. It was just one room with a bed and a small table with two chairs and a small cooking area and a bath in the back. She poured two beers and invited him to sit on the bed. Soon they were kissing each other and she started to take off his clothes. When she got to his underclothing, Savery felt an uncontrollable urge and he ejaculated all over himself, the bed and Nina. They were both very shocked but

Nina got a towel and wiped everything off and they just lay there and cuddled. After a while she showed him a very old worn out picture of a group of people and then started uncontrollably crying. Eventually the sergeant just left and went to his room for the night. The next morning he asked Horst about her.

"You didn't sleep with her, did you?" he asked.

"No," said Savery, "but I was tempted."

"Good; her life is complicated enough," said Horst.

"What do you mean? Why does she drink and cry so much?"

"She's very lonely. She misses her family."

"Where are they?" Savery asked.

"Most of them are dead," answered Horst. "Only her aunt is still alive and they haven't talked for years."

"How strange! Why not?" asked Savery.

"Because she lives in the village across the border. They can only wave handkerchiefs at each other."

Eventually Horst and Gabriela told Nina's story. They had all three gone to the same school in the village across the border. In the immediate years after the war the border was just a line. But by 1948 the Soviets started putting up barriers and the first of these was just a single line of barbed wire. Watching this happen caused both Horst and Gabriela to stay on the western side of the line but Nina's family continued to live in the village. Soon it became much more difficult to cross the border and more and more Easterners were trying to escape. By 1956, when Nina was twenty-two years old, her family decided that they too had to leave but it was too late. The barbed wire fence was bigger and the border guards too many. Still her family was convinced that they could make it. They secretly observed the guards, watched their schedules, got barbed wire cutters, and even made friends with some border guards. And then came that fateful night. The whole family, her father, her mother, her two sisters, her two uncles, her aunt, even her grandmother secretly made their way to the jumping off point. They actually made it across the final hundred meters to the fence and frantically cut a small hole through it when, crawling through, somehow one of them tripped a flare and the border guards came running, shooting their machine guns as they came. When it was over and the firing stopped, only Nina had made it safely through. All of her family lay dead on the ground, except for one aunt who was dragged off by the guards. Ever since that time Nina had lived here in the Gasthaus. She worked as a waitress at the inn for her board and room and eventually got a job at the VW plant. She was devastated. For three years she did not hear from her aunt. But then one afternoon five years ago Nina saw someone waving a white handkerchief from the village. Nina got binoculars from Horst and recognized her aunt. Since that day, every day at six pm Nina and her aunt waved handkerchiefs at each other across the border. "She's been carrying this around with her for years; she can't get over it," Horst concluded.

Although Nina heard that Horst had told Savery about her past, she never again brought up the subject. The sergeant continued to flirt with Nina, to speak German with her but never went back to her apartment. Horst told him one night, that he thought the sergeant was a symbol for Nina of the stability and happiness, which she could never have.

In the meantime one of the .1's at the site had discovered an interesting high level Russian signal. It had just suddenly appeared a few evenings before and then continued every night since. The signal was over modulated, coming in strongly and then fading out, then strongly again. All in all it did not seem at all military so he did not tape it. He was sure, however, that it was Russian. One night he taped it and Savery listened to it but it was so weak that he couldn't make sense out of it. They decided to look for it every evening just for fun. Although mostly illegible, it seemed like a speech about the military, while not being a military transmission.

The first week flew by and the second was almost done and Sergeant Savery felt right at home in Bahrdorf at the inn, "Zum weissen Spargel." He was wondering when Sergeant Krastner would be returning and how life would be back in Kassel after these two awesome weeks. He actually was starting to regret going back to headquarters, when he received a telephone call at the site from Captain Baer on the encoded line.

"How do you like it in Bahrdorf?" asked the captain.

"I love it, sir. I seem to fit right in."

That's what I've heard; everyone at the site is happy with you. Are you functioning OK at the 'Spargel'? Horst and Gabriela are great people; been through a lot too."

"You call it the 'Spargel' too. I really like it there but why are you calling, sir?"

"I just learned today that Krastner is coming back the day after tomorrow. His father made an amazing recovery. That means that you will not be needed there anymore."

Sergeant Savery's heart sank. Would this mean back to headquarters in Kassel?

"I've got a new assignment for you, Sergeant?"

"Back at headquarters?" asked Savery.

"No, actually something unexpected has come up and I feel you're just the person for the job. The Soviets have started some sort of exercises near the Brocken, highly unusual at this time of year. That's the highest mountain in the Harz Mountains and is just over the border from St. Andreasberg. We're sending up a contingency of about 20 soldiers to help figure out what they're up to. We'll set up an encampment on a mountain called Rehberg just outside of St. Andreasberg. We expect their signal to come in five by five so we should pick up some good intelligence. Are you interested?"

"Yes, sir. I'm really interested. I like it fine here, but I've heard St. Andreasberg is awesome. What's the time line, sir?" At the same time Savery was thinking of his NATO exercise encampment.

"You'll leave Bahrdorf tomorrow morning. Someone will take you to the 0800 train in Helmstedt and you will be back here by

1200 hours, just in time for the group orientation. By noon, the day after tomorrow, you'll be in St. Andreasberg."

"I'll have to tell Horst and Gabriela," said Savery.

"I've already told them and, besides, they're used to soldiers coming and going."

The conversation lasted a few more minutes and Savery was already missing the "Spargel" and even Nina.

Later that evening as he said farewell to her, she continually hugged him and openly cried.

IV

At 0700 the next morning Savery was standing in front of the inn waiting for his ride to the Helmstedt train station as the jeep pulled up. The driver hopped out to help when suddenly the two soldiers recognized each other.

"Rich?"

"Bill?"

"What are you doing here?"

"What are YOU doing here; I never expected to see you here."

The two soldiers shook hands and gave each other a hug. They had known each other since the first day of Russian school in Monterey more than two-and-a-half years ago. Rich had left after the first 48 weeks and Savery had gone on to the 75 week course. During those 48 weeks they had been the best of friends and they had experienced many adventures together. Savery remembered how Rich was always trying to impress girls. He was only 18 years old, six feet tall, good looking and very outgoing. He could charm anyone and had guts. Once he put his hand on a restaurant table and had allowed a Monterey college student to burn his hand with a cigarette just to impress the student's girlfriend. The smell of burning flesh had caused the restaurant owner to come over and end the situation by kicking everyone out. Rich was also extremely intelligent and had graduated from high school at age sixteen. When Rich finished the

48-week Russian course and was shipped out, he sold Savery his 1955 Ford Fairlane, which enabled him to have many more adventures.

"Did you keep working for Ruben Tice?" asked Rich.

"Of course," responded Bill. "A great guy and great inventor. I met a lot of people through him."

"How about the girl at Gilroy Hot Springs: the one with the pet tarantulas?"

"I drove up there a couple times but I was too busy to get involved and the spiders scared me," said Savery.

The two friends stood in the parking lot and talked for ten minutes before they finally got in the jeep and drove off.

"Richard Williams, you're a SPC-6. How did you pull that off?"

"Just doing my job. I see you're already a SPC-5."

"I just got lucky. I was in the right place at the right time."

They were still chatting about the old days as they passed the barracks at Grasleben, when, unexpectedly, Williams turned into a driveway. Out of a doorway of the house came a young eighteen-year-old girl, who came up to the jeep and said "Guten Morgen, Liebchen" to Williams, who then told Savery that he needed fifteen minutes alone with the girl and for Savery to take a walk. Dumbfounded the SPC-5 got out and walked some fifty meters away, when he noticed that the girl had climbed into the jeep and that the jeep was rocking back and forth. Savery just stared in disbelief. A few minutes later she climbed back out of the jeep and went back into the house. As Savery got back into the jeep, Williams waved goodbye to the girl and drove back out onto the highway heading toward Helmstedt.

"Just something I had to do," said Williams.

"Do you do that a lot?" asked Savery.

"I'm here to have fun and I'm having it."

"How many girls have you had?" asked the sergeant.

"I don't know, maybe fifty or sixty," said Williams.

"Fifty or sixty!" blurted out Savery.

"I'm not the same guy you knew back at Monterey. I picked up German over here really fast and I'm really enjoying life." Savery suddenly thought that he too should learn more German.

A few minutes later Rich dropped the SPC-5 off at the train station and drove off. Savery wondered where Williams was going. He hadn't even asked him where he was stationed or where he was living. On the trip back to Kassel he thought back to Bahrdorf, the "Spargel," Horst and Gabriela and Nina and he thought of the old days with Rich in Monterey, where Rich was definitely not the same guy and he wondered if he would ever see any of them again.

By early evening the orientation was over and Savery decided to go to the "Stern" with Cromby and Rolland. Cummings and Gehrlach were there talking to some girls. All four sat together at a long table and soon every seat was full. Savery had his dictionary out and was flipping pages as fast as he could, looking for German words. Lotte seemed impressed by Savery's eagerness to learn more German. The next morning the small group of soldiers convoyed their way to St. Andreasberg. This was the first time that the sergeant had been to the Harz Mountains and the entire trip was very scenic and reminded him of his home in Vermont. They took the Autobahn to Roringen just north of Göttingen and then drove thirty kilometers north east along a small road through several picturesque villages to Herzberg and then some twenty five more kilometers along a very narrow winding road higher and higher into the mountainous region. Finally they burst out of the dense forest to see a wide panorama of an open bowl of grassland, the opposite half rim of which was a town.

"St. Andreasberg, the most beautiful town in Germany!" the driver said. "You'll like this place!"

"I like it already!" Savery responded.

As they drove on around the rim, it became evident just how beautiful the town was. It was more than a kilometer long and seemed to have only one main street and was seldom wider than two hundred meters. Right in the center was the town square with a town hall, a library, and a church and all along the main street were many tourist shops, restaurants, cafes, bakeries and pastry shops. A few hundred meters after going through the center, Savery saw why the place looked so alive. It was a ski area! But unlike his hometown St. Andreasberg was at the top of the ski area and the runs went down from the town into the bowl, one right from the center of town. There were at least six lifts spread out through the town so the town seemed inviting and welcoming. Even though it was not yet ski season, the town was swarming with tourists so seemed much bigger than it probably actually was.

The convoy did not stop in the town but continued another kilometer, where, after passing by some kind of a school, it turned to the right along what appeared to be a logging road. It proceeded another half kilometer up hill and stopped at a clearing with an incredible view to the east. In the distance some fifteen kilometers away was a mountain which dwarfed the surroundings.

"The Brocken!" came the answer with a hand gesture in that direction before Savery could even ask the question. "We have a great view of them and they have a great view of us. Their radio signals will come in perfectly right here. The game continues."

It took the rest of the daylight hours just to get the basics set up. The mess tent seemed to be the most important but the pup tents were also high on the list. Savery shared a tent with Corporal Bryant, a communications specialist. That first night was really cold, so cold that Savery got up in the night and put on his uniform shirt and trousers and crawled back into his sleeping bag. In the morning shaving with warm water, heated in his helmet over a Sterno flame, was also an adventure. He had not experienced this since the NATO exercises and he found himself praising electricity. Of course, he reminded himself, it was already November and they were at a high elevation.

During the morning hours they got the generators running and started listening in to the Soviets on the radio. Captain Baer had been right; the signal came in five by five, crystal clear. Because there was no backlog, Savery went from one recording station to the next, listening in on as many live conversations as he could. It appeared to be a normal exercise. "They're probably having an exercise just to force us to be here freezing in this weather," suggested Pfc. Gracy. Everyone laughed but some probably felt that he was correct in his assumption.

By the end of the second day their existence on the mountain was getting a little boring, but things were about to pick up. It was payday! Payday was always the best day of the month. About noon a jeep came up the logging road. It contained a heavily armed driver and the paymaster, carrying the cash to pay all the soldiers from officers to privates. But even better than this, each soldier could get any amount of his pay in German currency at the standard rate of four Marks to the dollar. Soon everyone was lining up to receive his money. Lieutenant Silver, officer in charge, reminded everyone to guard his money well.

"SPC-5 Savery," said Savery when he got to the paymaster.

After looking on a list, the paymaster said: "Your pay is $300. How would you like it?"

"150 in dollars; the rest in Marks, please," answered Savery. He thought back to his last paycheck in security school just before leaving for Germany. His monthly paycheck had been $126. It was good, being a sergeant. The paymaster counted out a mountain of German money, 600 German marks. Back in his pup tent Savery recounted the money.

Then came the problem of guarding his money. He decided to carry it on his person twenty four hours a day just like the other soldiers did. Later that day started the rumors about a big card game after the evening meal in the mess tent. Everyone was talking about it and everyone seemed to have taken part in one before. Although he seldom had ever played poker, the sergeant was curious and decided to attend if only to watch. Besides, there was nothing else to do in the darkness.

At about 8 o'clock soldiers started appearing out of the darkness into the light of the mess tent. Eventually about 15 soldiers showed up and, after a brief discussion of the rules: five card draw, a five dollar ante, a five dollar raise limit, three games started. Savery and a couple others just looked on. After a half hour someone dropped out and Savery took his seat. At first everything went fine, Savery won a few bucks and lost a few bucks. At some point a player suggested that they change the game to seven card draw, add a wild card into each hand and things still went ok but eventually, special rules were added every few hands; the ante went up to $20 and the raise limit disappeared, the number of wild cards allowed increased to three and the number of cards that counted went from five to seven. At the same time most players dropped out of the game so that there were only five players left. Corporal Bryant warned Savery to get out of the game but Savery was having too much fun to quit.

Then came the fateful game. The 2's, 3's and 4's were wild. Savery looked at his first five cards; two kings, a pair of deuces, and an ace. He threw in the necessary fifty bucks to stay in the game. He discarded the ace and drew one card, a three. He bet $20. Everyone matched his bet, in the draw he received a four, he passed as a decoy but saw the $30 raise. His seventh and last card was a king. His heart pounded: six kings! A player across from him bet $200. $200, what can he have? thought the sergeant: he's bluffing. The next two players dropped out leaving only Savery to see or raise or drop out. Savery was convinced that he had already won and searched in his pockets for money. He had only $50 and his 600 Marks. After a brief hesitation he threw it all in. The player across the table showed his cards, a deuce, three 3's, two 4's and one ace: six aces! Savery was devastated. He stared in disbelief! He had lost all his money! He abruptly stood up and raced out into the darkness.

He wandered around in the darkness for over an hour but eventually the cold got to him and he found his way to his pup tent. "I told you to quit the game," said Corporal Bryant.

"What will I do now? I'm broke," said the sergeant.

"Sleep on it; everything is better in the sunlight."

But he did not sleep at all that night but rather relived the game over and over and decided to never again play cards for money.

At breakfast the next morning Savery realized that seven of the card players from the night before were present. After eating, they all told the sergeant to stay and play a hand of five-card poker. He did not want to but they repeatedly insisted. Each was dealt five cards; Savery had only two deuces. A player bet $20, and every other player matched it. "Savery will be $20 light," said Corporal Bryant from the side. Each player drew two cards. Savery's best hand was still two deuces. The winner from the night before, sitting to the right of Savery, bet 400 Marks. Everyone in turn around the table folded. The sergeant wanted to fold too but the player who had just bet told him to stay.

"But I have no money," exclaimed the sergeant.

"Just be light!" said the player. Confused, he said he would be 400 Marks light.

"What do you have?" asked the player.

"A pair of deuces," answered Savery.

"Beats me!" said the player and tossed his cards in.

"What?" said Savery, realizing what had just happened. A huge boulder had just been taken off his chest. His faith in his fellow man had been restored and Corporal Bryant had been right; things look better in the daylight.

As a result of the morning card game, the nine soldiers would become the very best of friends. Their first excursion together would happen that very night after a very happy, positive eight hours of duty, during which absolutely nothing of importance was learned from listening to the Russians.

A few soldiers decided to go into St. Andreasberg that very night; it was after all Saturday. A walking path crossed the logging road back down the mountain near the school. It continued through the woods behind the school all the way into town. The entire distance was less than one and a half kilometers making it a very easy walk. After dinner the soldiers, having cleaned up as much as possible and having put on civilian clothing, ventured forth on their hike into town. On the lawn of the school was a sign, which read "St. Andreasberg Internat" which turned out to mean international boarding school and in the lighted dormitory windows many teenage students could be seen moving around.

As they walked toward the downtown area, they agreed to be on their best behavior and not to get into any confrontations; they were here to enjoy. Right near the center of town was a big club with the neon sign "Weltall." From the club was coming modern German music, so the group decided to go in. Inside, the place was huge and very modern with a long bar, a huge dance floor and at least 25 tables, and, most surprising of all, a live five-person band. There were at least thirty other guests in the club and most of them were late teenagers or in their early twenties. The group occupied two tables, and Savery, still happy about his good fortune ordered a beer for each of them. Somehow someone got into a conversation with one of the Germans and before you knew it, everyone was in one big group talking to each other. For at least one hour everyone was totally happy conversing in English and German all mixed together. The male Germans did not seem upset that the American soldiers were talking to their female friends. By the end some soldiers even danced with German girls. Sergeant Savery found one girl especially nice and attractive and he talked to her as much as he could. She was exactly his height, had light skin and jet black hair in a braded ponytail, which hung down almost to her knees. Her hair drove him wild and he just wanted to talk to her and for some reason she just smelled good. They even danced once to the song "Komm, gib' mir deine

Hand" but he was very careful not to actually touch her; he did not want to scare her away. By 10 pm most of the young Germans had left and the American soldiers were alone. After two more rounds of beer they all walked back together. They talked the entire way back about how great it was in the club, about how pretty the German girls were and about how friendly all the German "kids" were and they decided to do the same thing on the next Saturday night.

As the week went on, life in the Rehberg encampment was very constant, the Russians were radio-active only during the daytime and seldom had a single transmission during the night. It was suggested that in the evening they were probably also at their own club talking with East German teenagers. On the American side, headquarters was happy with the work being done and just wanted the group to keep up the good work.

Some soldier reported at breakfast on Tuesday morning, that he had heard somewhere that just down the road a few kilometers in the direction of the border and away from St. Andreaberg there was a very small village with a cool Gasthaus. The village, Oderhausen, had only nine or ten houses and thus was hardly on any map. It was decided to visit the Gasthaus the following night. Because they didn't have transportation, it was decided to hitchhike there in groups of two. Therefore two soldiers at a time stood at the entrance to the logging road, hitchhiking, while the rest hid out of view. When two got a ride, two more appeared and took their place. Eventually all ten made their way to Oderhausen and its only Gasthaus, the "Kuh." When the first soldiers arrived there were only the bartender, a woman of about thirty, and three twenty-year-old girls in the "Kuh." By the time that all 10 soldiers had arrived there were another five young females but no males except for the American soldiers. The soldiers decided to have a good time and started to drink beer after beer. The juke box was blasting German songs with an occasional English song thrown in. Savery kept playing "Nowhere Man" and got so drunk, that he didn't know where he was and he passed out.

He suddenly awoke from the silence which surrounded him. It was jet black and he literally could not see his hand in front of his face. By stretching out his hands, he found one wall and then another and then something in the middle. "What the . . . a toilette?!" he mumbled to himself. "Am I in a bathroom?"

"Hey, can anybody hear me?" he called out loud and then in German, "Ist jemand da?" But no one answered; he was all alone. He found his way to his feet and tried to open the bathroom door but it was bolted from the other side. After a few moments of confusion, he forced open the window and climbed out into the darkness. He remembered the direction he was traveling when he arrived here and started walking in the opposite direction to get home. Hours later, having not seen a single vehicle, he arrived at the logging road, climbed the hill and lay down in his pup tent just as the sun was coming up. Corporal Bryant was not there and Savery wondered where he was. Three soldiers came back even later than Savery and the lieutenant was upset with all ten soldiers. But, boy, did they have some stories and none believed Savery when he said he had passed out in the toilette. They all knew he was hiding something. The next three days were not fun; the lieutenant was very hyper.

By Saturday everything was going better and the same ten soldiers walked back into St. Andreasberg, past the same international school, to the same club "Weltall," where the same group of young Germans was already there, enjoying the same music. Half way through the evening someone remarked that this sure was a different group than at the Gasthaus in Oderhausen. It was truly another awesome night. Sergeant Savery talked with everyone and danced once again with the same beautiful girl with the long black hair. She told him her name was Katia and Savery told her his name was Bill. That was it. For some reason Savery just wanted to be with her, in her presence, nothing else seriously entered his mind.

On Sunday afternoon Bryant and the sergeant took a leisurely walk into town. Even though it was just above freezing, the sun was out and the streets were full of people. From a block away they smelled a delicious aroma coming from a pastry shop and they decided to go in, have a cup of coffee, and eat a piece of pastry. The sign on the front read "Kaufmanns Konditorei." They entered the building and approached the display case.

"Kann ich Ihnen helfen?" asked a lady of about forty.

"Do you speak English? Ik sprecke nix deutsch," said Bryant.

"Meine Tochter spricht Englisch; ich hole sie." And with that she went into a back room. When she came back, Katia was with her!

"Katia!" said Savery.

"Bill!" said Katia.

"What are you doing here, Katia?

"I live here. This is my mother."

"Frau Kaufmann!" said Katia's mother and extended her hand to Savery.

"Savery, Bill Savery," said the sergeant. "I'm with the soldiers up on Rehberg. This is Bryant." Savery suddenly realized that he did not know Bryant's first name.

"John, John Bryant," said Bryant and extended his hand toward Frau Kaufmann.

"My daughter has told me a lot about you; she has seen you at the 'Weltall'."

"Would you like a cup of coffee?" asked Katia. "And some of our best pastry?"

"Yes, something you made," said Savery.

"I'll bring you our famous house Käsekuchen, I think you say cheese cake. It's very well liked."

A couple minutes later Savery and Bryant were enjoying the cheese cake, the coffee and the ambiance and the wonderful aroma of pastry. Katia came and sat with them for ten minutes with her flower-covered hands and her mother kept looking in on the conversation. Just before Katia had to go back to work, she asked Savery if he could be at the Konditorei at 6 a.m. the following morning to do something fun and he promised that he would be there.

Bryant and Savery stayed in St. Andreasberg for an additional two hours and visited several shops and even the library but their conversation kept coming back to Katia and her Konditorei. They kept speculating about what fun thing Katia was referring and Bryant kept saying that he wanted to come along, while Savery kept saying that he could not.

At 5 a.m. the next morning his wind up alarm clock went off and Savery dragged himself out of his sleeping bag. It was brutally cold but somehow he managed to warm up some water, to wash up, brush his teeth and shave. He put on civilian clothing but also added his lined fatigue jacket. By 5:30 he was on his way to town. He arrived at the pastry shop around ten minutes before six and could see lights coming from the back rooms. He didn't know if he should knock on the door so he just decided to wait outside. At about 6 a.m. Katia appeared from behind the building, pulling a small wagon.

"Guten Morgen, Bill. Schön, dass du schon hier bist," she said as she extended her hand in greeting.

"Morning," said Savery, "What are you pulling?"

"Rolls; we call them Brötchen. We are going to deliver them to houses around the town. I hope you want to do this with me."

"Of course I do; I think it will be fun. Who baked the rolls?"

My mother and father just did and they're still warm. The shop will be open in a half hour."

With that they started their trek through the town. As they went along a side street, Savery became aware of the sound of a small bell attached to the wagon that rang every time they went over a bump. "The bell is mostly meant as a greeting for our customers when we approach their house in the darkness, some people wait inside their door to hear the bell and then open their door and greet us. But normally we place their rolls in a paper bag, leave the rolls on their door step and ring their doorbell as we leave. Our first customer is

Dr. Kranz; he lives just down the street. He gets eight rolls every morning." She stopped in the darkness, took eight rolls out of the big sack of rolls on the wagon and placed them in a paper bag. At the doctor's house, she put down the rolls, rang the doorbell and proceeded down the street.

A few seconds later came a voice from behind them saying "Danke, Katia." And so it went on for about an hour. They arrived back at the pastry shop just as it started to get light. They had delivered all the rolls. Savery had been in awe of her beauty and wholesomeness and now he was in awe of the way she interacted with the customers and the way she customers loved her. He felt very fortunate to be with her.

"Well, what do you think? Do you want to do this tomorrow?" she asked. "I do this every day."

"Absolutely, I'll be here!" he answered. "But there's just one thing."

"Yes, what Bill?"

"I want to learn to speak German. I want to speak German with you or at least try. Will you speak German with me?"

"And I want to learn to speak English better."

They decided that Bill would try to speak more German, no matter how bad it was, and that Katia would continue to speak English as much as she wanted, while gently correcting Bill's German. A good compromise. They shook hands as they parted. On the walk back up the mountain Savery thought that he could fall in love with this girl.

At breakfast several soldiers were eagerly waiting to learn what the fun was, to which Savery answered: "We delivered rolls."

"That was the 'fun'?" one soldier sarcastically laughed. But he had no idea.

For the next two weeks Savery helped deliver rolls every morning and also saw Katia at the "Weltall" on Saturday nights. He was becoming more and more attached to her and everyone noticed.

Even those who didn't, still noticed that he was always trying to speak German.

As luck and nature would have it, the weather became increasingly colder and there came the day when it snowed and the snow did not melt. To make things worse the Soviets got sick of the weather too and moved back into winter quarters probably across from Schöningen. The rumors started flying that the encampment would soon end and so it happened that on one frosty morning all soldiers were called together to get the news that at 1000 the following morning they too would all leave St. Andreasberg for Kassel.

Despite the fact that he knew it would happen, despite the fact that winter had begun and despite the fact that he had never even kissed Katia, Savery was devastated. That night he walked alone into St. Andreasberg to tell her that they were leaving but she had already heard it. Bad news travels fast. They stood there in the darkness outside the Konditorei and hugged each other and both cried. Savery wondered why it always seemed that he had to leave every place he really liked.

V

Six weeks passed. Everything seemed to be in slow motion. The Soviets seemed to be in slow motion too and there was never much work to do in the Ice House. Every Friday and Saturday night in the "Stern" the usual soldiers and the usual girls gathered, flirted and got drunk. Somehow it was not as alluring to Sergeant Savery as it had been just a short time ago. He found himself thinking back on St. Andreasberg and Katia. He had tried to call her a couple times but did not get through. He had even tried to find a ride up to see her but after much indecision on the part of the driver that had fallen through. He did notice that several soldiers had cars and he thought that he should have his own car. Then he could see Katia on any weekend.

Christmas had come and gone; New Year's the same. Nothing could get him cheered up and he started to drink more than his normal two beers. He friends noticed the increase and often poked fun of him, if only in a friendly way. And then one morning in mid-January Captain Baer called him into his office.

"Is everything OK?" the captain asked.

"What do you mean, sir?" responded the sergeant.

"You don't seem as cheery as you've always been."

"Everything's fine, sir. I just miss St. Andreasberg and the people there."

"And some girl, no doubt," noted the captain. "Don't worry, Sergeant. You'll get over it."

"I hope so," added the sergeant. "Why am I here, sir?"

"Believe it or not, I have just the medicine you need. A trip up to Gartow. Do you know where it is, Sergeant?"

"Gartow, I think it's way up north, near Hamburg isn't it?"

"Correct. It's deep in the British zone. Do you want to go up there?"

"Why, sir? For how long?"

"The 318th wants its presence there noticed by our brass so at least once a year normally in the winter we go up there and mingle with the natives as we say. We work with the British observing the Soviets and just relax and have a good time. We stay a week to ten days."

"Do I have to sleep in a pup tent, sir? It's cold outside."

"Believe it or not, no. We stay at the only Gasthaus in Gartow, the 'Seehund'." I know the owners well, good people. Already got reservations. Only four of you will be going. You already know the other three: Baker, Cummings, and Gehrlach. Yes or no, Sergeant; make up your mind."

"If we'll get warm showers," Savery laughed, "I'm in."

"Oh, yes, one more thing. You'll have to drive a communications truck but you've done that before. You and Baker in the truck and Cummings and Gehrlach in a jeep."

Savery thought of the last time he saw Baker in a communications truck and he expected to have a smoother experience this time. And Cummings and Gehrlach were really good guys too.

Three days later at 0800 they were on the Autobahn headed north. They stopped near Hannover for a cup of coffee and then exited the Autobahn and went northeast 50 kilometers to Celle and then another75 kilometers to north east Uelzen. There they stopped at a roadside German Gasthaus for lunch and tanked up at a British base. Finally they drove the last 75 kilometers north east to Gartow.

These final 75 kilometers had been on very narrow and rough country roads with very little traffic. The towns were very small; some took only a moment to drive through. It became evident that Gartow was very far off the beaten path. Savery was surprised that there was no snow on the ground and Gehrlach explained that this was because of the salt air. They were so close to the North Sea that it seldom snowed here, but rather rained. In fact it was a very dark day, indicating a wet day approaching.

There was no one to meet them, when they pulled into the Gasthaus "zum Seehund," which literally meant the seadog. They secured their belongings and went in to register and were greeted by a young married couple Sylvia and Thorsten, the owners.

"How's Captain Baer?" asked Thorsten in perfect English.

"He sends his greetings," said Savery. "He said you were good people."

"He stayed here once for three months."

Cummings and Gehrlach checked in, speaking only German.

"Thorsten, Sylvia, wir sehen uns schon wieder!"

"Jawohl, alte Freunde, Grüss euch!" and they gave each other a big hug.

"How do you know each other?" asked Savery.

"Because we were here last fall."

"Where was I? I didn't know you were here."

"You were in Bahrdorf," came the response.

Each soldier got a second floor single room with a view to the back. From the windows one could see the border with its death strip in the distance. In the hall there was a bathroom for women and another bath for men. There were also two showers. They were going to like this place. After bringing their luggage to the rooms, they emptied the jeep and locked the communications truck. They then had a beer at the bar and then another and then still another. Finally they all ate Schweinerippchen, the house specialty for the night. After dinner they chatted with each other and with a couple of young German males who wandered in and finally Savery crashed for the night. The other three sat at the bar and eventually some young Germans, whom Gehrlach and Cummings knew from last year, came in and the three soldiers stayed up until the Gasthaus closed for the night.

At 0800 they all went down for breakfast and discussed what they would do for the day.

Let's let our presence be known to the Soviets," said Gehrlach. "Let's drive down to the river's edge."

"Great idea!" answered Cummings, "Do you think they've missed us? I have an idea. Let's do what we did to them the last day we were here. Let's ignore them."

Outside, Baker started to unlock the truck but Gehrlach said not to, that they would walk to the river. Gehrlach had a baseball with him, which he had bought in the PX in Kassel. He gently tossed it as they walked along the parking lot and then across the road down a side pathway. Ahead Savery could see a ridge about eight meters high which extended out of sight from left to right. When they got to it, they climbed to the top. On the other side was a wide river going out of sight in both directions and on the other side were people in some kind of uniform.

"Wow," said Baker. "What river is this?"

"Are you kidding? It's the Elbe."

"But the Elbe starts in the East and flows into the West. Who are those men over there across the river?"

"Can't you see them? They're Soviet and East German border guards."

"But they're only a hundred meters from us. Is it safe here? Where are we, in the East or in the West?"

"We are at a very special place, the only place along the entire 600 mile border where one side of a river is in the East and the other side is in the West. No barbed wire fence!"

"But looking out my window this morning I could see the border on the other side."

"This area is like a thumb sticking into East Germany from the West and Gartow is like the thumbnail, right at the tip."

"No wonder there are so few people here. Who would want to live here?!"

Eventually Savery and Baker calmed down and the four soldiers found a stick and started trying to play some baseball. They were well aware of the Soviets and East German guards watching them, some through field glasses. But the Americans totally ignored them; it was a fun game.

The rest of the day was spent walking up and down the bank of the river and just wandering through the village on the only road there was. By early evening they were back in the "Seehund" having a beer when the door opened and two very young girls walked in.

"Bernie, Dave!" they exclaimed as they ran up to Gehrlach and Cummings and hugged them. "Liese, Gabi!" yelled the two soldiers. And with that the four of them were off at a corner table intimately talking.

In fact they spent the entire evening together and at one time they even went up to the soldiers' rooms.

Savery and Bryant just sat there alone and wondered about the girls. They looked so young. Finally they asked Thorsten and Sylvia about the girls. They were told that the girls were students at the local GymnasIum or high school in Trebel and that they were sixteen years old.

"Sixteen, they're just kids," said Savery. "Should they be here and upstairs?"

"Actually, legally they're adults. They can do what they want!" said Sylvia. "There is nothing I can or want to do about it. It's all part of growing up."

By morning the girls had left and the four soldiers were having breakfast at the inn. Cummings and Gehrlach kept chuckling and grinning. They seemed to have had a very good night. As Savery was wondering exactly what they were supposed to be doing here, the door opened and in walked a British sergeant.

"Sorry I'm late," he said. "There was a mix up and we thought you were arriving today."

Sergeant McClanahan was a tall, good natured, red haired soldier attached to the British intelligence group in the northern West German border sector. His group did essentially exactly what the 318th did, listen to the Russians. "You will be working with us for the next few days, just to see how we do things. This will result in better cooperation and coordination in our efforts. Or at least we hope it will. Today we will drive to one of our reconnaissance sites near the village of Laase about fifteen kilometers northwest of here. It's right at the river's edge where we'll be face to face with Soviets. To some it's intimidating. To me it's exciting."

Within the hour they were following Sergeant McClanahan to Laase, where he took a sudden right turn and drove up over the same type ridge that they had visited the night before. Savery realized then that it was a levy built along the entire Elbe River probably to help prevent flooding. He wondered if the East German side had a levy too. On the other side of the levy were several British communications trucks along the river's edge. After parking their vehicles the Americans set up their equipment, just as they had in the NATO exercises. And soon they were gathering what little intelligence they could find. Most every Soviet and East German radio transmission involved the Americans. The border guards were trying to figure out exactly what they were up to on this side. It was a game! It looked dangerous but it was only a game. By late afternoon they folded up and drove to a British base, where they tanked up, and had a few drinks of British stout. Then they drove back to the "Seehund" for a delicious home cooked meal. Just after dinner the same two girls, Liese and Gabi, showed up and Cummings and Gehrlach were lost to another sleepless night.

At breakfast the two soldiers were once again in a very good mood. But Baker and Savery were not as happy and they decided to find something to do here. Because there seemed to be very few visitors to the inn, they asked Cummings and Gehrlach what else there was to do here. "Nothing," came their reply. "But not far from here, only two hours away is the massive city of Hamburg and there is always a lot going on twenty four hours a day there."

"But can we go there? We're supposed to be here in Gartow," said Savery.

"No problem, Captain Baer realized that we might need a break, so he filled out official two day long furlough papers for all four of us to Hamburg. He even gave us official permission to drive the jeep there. We just have to date them when we leave. There's just one restriction, no U-turns on the Reeperbahn."

Cummings laughed but Savery and Baker didn't get the joke. They all decided to drive to Hamburg on Saturday and spend the night. Thorsten had a friend there, who owned a Gasthaus so they had a place to stay.

The next few days were carbon copies of the first days. Working with the Brits was fun and Cummings and Gehrlach were two very happy soldiers. Sergeant Savery wondered if they would actually go to Hamburg or just stay here but in the end, they went, because they had promised and knew Hamburg so well.

Hamburg was jumping and the soldiers quickly centered in on the harbor district. There were thousands of men on the streets, some in uniforms that Savery had never seen before, there were merchant marines from all over the world and the sergeant remembered from an orientation that it was here that Soviet and US merchant marines came into the closest contact with merchandise, switching carriers for home ports. The four decided to stick together and more than once almost got into dangerous situations but they made it safely until late in the night when they arrived at the Reeperbahn, the red light district.

Part of the Reeperbahn was a brothel with forty or fifty houses side by side along a pedestrian-only 150 meter section of street. Each house front was lit up so that it appeared one was looking into a living room. In each living room there were girls, very beautiful young girls in great physical condition, many undoubtedly as young as eighteen. Each one was scantily clad and each one was extremely inviting. Walking along the street were hundreds of men, each searching for that one prefect sexual encounter. When one found that perfect someone, he would walk up to the living room, speak with the girl, and negotiate a price for whatever was expected. The man would accept the price and be led into the back or reject the price and rejoin the crowd looking for happiness. The walking street also had many policemen and MP's patrolling, guarding against violence, protecting the girls.

The four soldiers agreed to just wander up and down the street for a half hour, to take in the sites, to get a feel for what was going on, and to then meet and decide the next step. Wandering along, Savery found one very beautiful girl, who reminded him of Katia. She too had dark, long flowing hair and she was obviously very expensive because she did not exit into the back with anyone for the entire half hour, even though several men had talked to her. Savery realized that he had an erection just watching her. When they all met back together, everyone had a similar story.

"Well, what do you think, shall we partake?" asked Baker. "I'm for doing it."

"I'm for it too!" said Savery.

"I'll just look," said Cummings. "Things couldn't be better for me than they are right now."

"I'll abstain," said Gehrlach. "Gabi suits me just fine. But go ahead, boys, have some fun. That's why we're here."

The three of them walked along with Baker and he pointed out a beautiful girl with light blond, shoulder length hair. They all watched her for a while, boy, was she sexy, and after someone had failed in his negotiations with her, Baker succeeded and was led into the back. It was Savery's turn. "It's Katia!" said Savery, as he pointed her out. But they both had already seen her and determined that she was among the prettiest girls there. Savery approached her, talked a little with her, searched through his pockets, and then came back to his friends to borrow 200 Marks. He then went back and left into the back with her. But things did not go as he had planned. Although at first extremely turned on, he started thinking of all those other men who had probably made love to her this very night and he started thinking of Katia, to whom he was about to be unfaithful and he just couldn't do it. The girl, as beautiful as she really was, tried everything to get him involved but it was of no use. In all he was in the back with her for just fifteen minutes before he left out the side door and Gehrlach and Cummings were surprised that he was already done. Savery assured them that he had had a great time and that it was worth every Mark. It took Baker almost another forty minutes to finish his fun and he was very satisfied. "Does anybody know what 'Versager' means?" asked Savery, but no one did. It wasn't in his small dictionary.

By the next afternoon they were back in the "Seehund," when Gabi and Liese arrived directly from school. Within twenty minutes they were already upstairs for the night. Sometimes life didn't seem fair. Baker, on the other hand, was in the greatest of moods.

Eventually the stay came to an end. Cummings had managed to have Captain Baer extend the stay to three complete weeks and had tried for a fourth but with no success. And so it came that they found themselves on the way back to Kassel. Sergeant Savery found himself looking back at this stay and he truly regretting not making love to the prostitute, she was so incredibly beautiful. He wished he could have a second opportunity. Cummings and Gehrlach were also very quiet along the way. They had undoubtedly just had the best three weeks of their lives. Only Baker was vocal the entire trip. For him, too, it had been a great trip. Savery wished he had noted the restriction on his furlough papers; he sincerely wished he had not taken a U-turn on the Reeperbahn.

VI

O nce again life at headquarters was boring. Captain Baer sensed something was wrong and he continually tried to cheer Sergeant Savery up.

"So how was it in Gartow?" he asked. "Not much going on there?"

"It was OK, I liked the Brits," he responded. "Sergeants Gehrlach and Cummings knew their way around."

"And how was Hamburg? A lot of merchant marines there; it can be a dangerous place!"

"It was OK but too busy for me."

"So everything was just OK? I sent you up for a reason. Sometimes there are incidents up there because of the border and, you never know, some day we might have to send you there for a real reason."

In late February Captain Baer again called Savery to his office and the sergeant thought it was for another pep talk.

"The 318th prides itself on moral, Sergeant, and I feel you are not happy here."

"It's OK, sir. Just not much going on."

"So I've decided to permanently transfer you back up to Bahrdorf. You'll be close to the border, close to the action. You're already the best Russian .3 we have and we need someone like you up there. What do you say? Are you interested?"

"I've heard rumors, that Bahrdorf is closing," said Savery. "Any truth to that?"

"I've heard that same rumor, and you never know what the brass will come up with, but nothing yet that I know of."

"Where will I be staying, at the 'Spargel'?"

"No, Sergeant, there's room in the weapons factory in Grasleben. You'll be staying there. Besides, I hear there's an old friend of yours living there."

"Who's that, sir?

"Sergeant Williams."

"Rich? Is that where he's living? But he doesn't work at Bahrdorf, does he? I didn't see him at all until the day I left."

"No, he works in Schöningen a little farther south but he prefers living in Grasleben, close to the night life in Helmstedt. And he has his own car. He can use a good friend now; he's done some strange things recently. So, do you want the assignment or not?"

"Yes, sir, and thank you."

"You'll be leaving for Helmstedt on the 1000 military train tomorrow. Pack all your gear. I'll have your orders to you before you leave."

At 10 a.m. Sergeant Savery was on the train, but this time it was overfull with soldiers, all headed for duty in Berlin. He was the only person to get out in Helmstedt. Once again he was met at the station by the same driver, who took him to the border crossing and then on to Grasleben. Savery wondered if the detour was standard procedure. But he enjoyed seeing Checkpoint Alpha again; it brought Savery back to reality.

It was clear why everyone referred to the barracks in Grasleben as a weapons factory. Quite simply it looked like and was an old bomb factory with four huge halls full of bunk beds with adjoining shower and bath facilities. Each bed had a locker for clothes and personal items. Otherwise there was nothing. In the back there was a huge parking lot half full of cars, many of which looked to be junk. Why would anyone want to live here? the sergeant thought. There were a couple empty bunk beds in one hall and Savery was told to select one. There seemed to be no one in charge, no security, no kitchen, no anything. It seemed to Savery that he was totally isolated.

Eventually after looking around again, he got a ride to the site in Bahrdorf and spent two hours getting reacquainted with the crew. At the end of the shift some soldiers were going for dinner at the "Spargel" and he went along; after all, he was stranded and he needed a ride plus he secretly hoped to see Nina. But she wasn't there. According to Horst, she was working the evening shift at the VW plant in Wolfsburg. When he finally climbed into bed he was totally depressed and wondered how he had gotten into this mess.

The next morning he was hungry and could not figure out where to eat. Finally he asked a corporal and was told, "There's no food here but just down the road around the corner is a farmhouse. The owners serve us any meal whenever we want. They're trying to open up a real Gasthaus and are building up their reserves. Of course we are within walking distance from Checkpoint Alpha about one kilometer through the woods. Just follow the path but be careful; don't get too close to the death strip. The checkpoint has a 24-hour restaurant, anyway half the troops living here work at the crossing so you can always get a ride. Just ten minutes farther away is Helmstedt and that is always hopping."

"I still don't get it; why do they want us to stay here and not, say, at the 'Spargel'?"

"Because the US military owns the factory and therefore does not have to pay the soldiers for off base housing. They just have to pay a food allotment. It's a matter of saving money."

"And why do soldiers want to live here?" asked the sergeant. "It's not exactly fancy!"

"For several reasons including total freedom, lack of supervision, an occasional wild party, girls and no officers!" Savery was not convinced but decided to give it a shot. He realized that what he really needed was a car. And he discovered that one soldier, who owned a car, was being discharged. Savery bought the car, a fifteen-year-old VW Beetle, which the owner called his "Käfer" for one hundred Marks ($25).

But a funny thing happened out back in the parking lots. Savery was trying to learn how to drive stick shift, when there appeared another soldier doing in same in his newly bought Beetle. Before they knew it, on purpose or just by accident, the two vehicles collided, causing serious damage to both cars. Several soldiers heard the crash and came running. Soon they were chanting "Derby, derby, derby!" The two drivers got the hint and they started backing their cars toward each other, repeatedly bumping together until both cars would not move anymore.

"Boy, was that fun!" exclaimed Savery as the two soldiers shook hands, the crowd cheered and two more cars were added to the many wrecked vehicles in the parking lot.

The following day another soldier got his orders back to the States and Savery had a second demolition derby; it was again a draw.

After about a week the sergeant got used to life at the bomb factory and actually started to enjoy being here. At least once every day he walked through the woods along the path to the border crossing and he was always very aware not to wander into the death strip. As the week went on, he regretted wrecking his two cars but it had been fun and had earned him a reputation as an OK guy. He finally found another departing soldier and bought his twelve-year-old "Kaefer" for a hundred Marks. Another $25! He was determined this time not to wreck it but to get license plates so he could actually drive it. It turned out to be really simple, he just had to fill out some papers at the PX in Helmstedt, take the car to a military inspection station and pay a fee for the plates plus the standard insurance charge. The entire process cost less than $50. Two days later he had his car.

One evening after Savery had just arrived at the bomb factory from Bahrdorf, who should be standing there but Rich Williams.

The two of them drove in Savery's car to Helmstedt for a beer in the "Haifisch" Gasthaus, where there were many US and British soldiers. Rich knew almost all of them and, to Savery's surprise, they all called him "Willi." For the past week Rich had written himself furlough papers, had somehow got them signed, and had driven up to Copenhagen to Tivoli Gardens.

"Four more," he said with a chuckle, "Teenage Swedish girls are hot."

"Copenhagen? Tivoli Gardens? Swedish girls? Isn't that Denmark?"

"Yes, but Tivoli Gardens is an amusement park for all of Scandinavia. It's swarming with girls. I prefer Swedish girls. They are naturally light blond and I mean all of them." Savery thought back to the jeep ride with Williams; that girl was blond too.

After a few beers Rich said that he wanted to visit some British soldier friends stationed at an intelligence base in Königslutter am Elm. Savery had never heard of the place but finally agreed to drive there. The road was dark and narrow and it was snowing but they made it there and spent several hours in some Gasthaus near the base and got very drunk. Savery decided he was too drunk to drive back and he didn't know the way so Rich got in the driver's seat and wildly drove away from the Gasthaus. Rich said he knew a short cut through some very small towns. Soon the two of them were singing a song Savery had heard a couple times in the "Stern" in Kassel. It included the words: "Fuck 'em all; fuck 'em all. Fuck the long, the short and the tall; fuck all the captains who like to give shit . . ." They were singing the refrain for about the fiftieth time racing through the night when they collided with a brick structure. The collision was in a village at a very sharp narrow corner and Rich had managed to hit just a glancing blow and the car was bounced back out onto the road and they just continued to sing and drive.

The next day, they sobered up and viewed the damage. The driver's side front bumper had been bent backward, the front fender was gone, the outside of the driver's door was twisted, the rear fender was gone and the back bumper was missing. Savery was very upset at Rich but Rich just laughed it off. They were fortunate to be alive. The next day they took William's car and search for the structure they had hit but they could not find it, they couldn't even identify the correct village.

Sergeant Savery needed another car!

When one soldier at Grasleben heard the story, he said laughingly "Willi the Bag strikes again!"

"Willi the Bag!" thought Savery. He had heard that name several times since he arrived in Germany. Willi the Bag was famous in stories in every soldier's bar. He was a symbol of chaos in an organized world, defying structure and order.

"Rich, why did they call you 'Willi' in the 'Haifisch' yesterday?" Savery asked.

"That's just what they call me, Willi, Willi the Bag. I think it's funny. I told you I'm not the same guy that I was in Monterey."

Sergeant Savery decided to avoid SPC-6 Williams for a while.

But, as things turned out, Savery and Williams were back together with the Brits in Königslutter a week later. They had got a ride there and were supposed to be picked up at midnight. They got really drunk. Rich was so drunk, that he kept falling down but he also kept drinking. At some point during the evening he stumbled and fell down on top of a potbelly stove in the corner. He screamed and tried up get off the red hot stove. The bartender came running, pulled him off and called a local doctor, who came to the bar to try to help. Williams just screamed. Eventually the doctor put some kind of salve on the side of Williams' face, and more salve on his hands, and wrapped his entire head and both hands in a white gauze to try to protect the wounds from infection. Williams looked like a mummy. At some point Williams insisted that he was OK and the doctor left. The bartender had paid the doctor.

But, as luck would have it, their ride home never came and Williams and Savery were stranded in Königslutter. At 1 a.m. Williams came up with a plan.

At approximately 2 a.m. every night the train to Berlin went through Königslutter. It didn't stop but had to go slowly because of some curves and an incline up ahead. They would just go up to this incline, wait for the train, hop on board and ride to Helmstedt and get off the train. They would avoid the conductor. Williams said he had done it before and that it was easy.

William bought a fifth of vodka, put it in a paper bag, and the two of them headed out to the incline just outside town in the forest. Soon the train came and they ran alongside it, caught hold of the door and swung themselves up into an empty car. Savery just wanted to hide there but Williams wanted to search through the train. In the second car back there was an old lady sleeping. As the soldiers were going past her, she woke up and was shocked to see the mummy carrying a paper bag. Startled, she asked in German what he was doing and he responded in German that he had a bomb and was going to blow up the train.

The lady stood up and hurried away in the opposite direction from where the soldiers were headed. Just before Helmstedt in a wooded area Williams pulled the emergency stop and the two soldiers jumped off the train and disappeared. An hour later they were in the bomb factory. "Another successful trip," said Williams, alias Willi the Bag.

A week went by and Williams' face and hands healed up and left no apparent scars. The doctor had known what he was doing. By the end of the week they were back in the "Haifisch" and Rich was surrounded by girls. Sergeant Savery heard some soldiers talking about a rumor and joined their conversation.

"When do you think it will happen?" One soldier was saying.

"What are you talking about?" interrupted Sergeant Savery.

"Haven't you heard? They're going to close down Bahrdorf?"

"What!?" Captain Baer just told me, that he had heard nothing about it."

"Well, it's happening."

"When have you heard that it will happen?" asked the sergeant.

"I think it's happening right now," came the response.

"What will happen with us?"

"Now that's a very good question."

Rich was not concerned at all. "In about a week I'm getting discharged and I'm going back to America. I don't care what they do." Savery thought back to his decision to enter the Russian 75-week course. Rich, who actually just barely qualified for the offer, had decided not to take it because he would have to stay in the army for and additional year. And now Rich was leaving and Savery had one year to go.

Three days later Captain Baer was in the site at Bahrdorf talking to the troops. "I know this is somewhat of a surprise, it even surprised me, but the brass has made the decision to close the base. We just don't gather enough intelligence here. It's not your fault. The Russians have just moved their operations south near the end of our intercept range so we're going to follow them. You will all be transferred within the next month, some to Kassel, some to Schöningen. We'll be ramping up the size of our operations there. In the meantime just continue your everyday duties. The barracks in Grasleben will remain open. The MP contingent will still be housed there and there's talk the Brits might be interested in housing some troops there too. We going to take out our best equipment from Bahrdorf and transport it to Berlin. They need all the equipment they can get their hands on with tensions there increasing as they are. Are there any questions?"

There were endless questions and the captain was very patient answering them all. At the end of the meeting, he pulled Sergeants Savery and Bush over to the side. "As I just said to the troops, we will be sending our best equipment to Berlin. I have decided that you two will be the ones to transport the equipment."

"What?" interrupted Savery. "We're going to Berlin?"

"Correct, Sergeant Savery. We feel both of you are very interested in the situation here and we feel you are both good drivers so we're going to have you drive the equipment to Berlin, see the sites, take a couple required seminars about the political situation and then return here to Grasleben. To be honest to you, we have not yet decided where you will then be stationed. Does that sound OK?"

"Yes, sir!" responded both soldiers together.

"When will that occur?" asked Bush.

"Tomorrow!" responded the captain. "You'll just need fatigues for four days and your personal hygiene items; you won't need any civilian clothing. We have already arranged for you to join a convoy and we'll be packing a communications truck chuck full of equipment later today and tonight. We'll have all the necessary paperwork. The military has even notified the Russians that another convoy is coming. You just have to be at Checkpoint Alpha at 0800 hours. One of you will drive a jeep and the other will drive the truck. Then after a couple days in Berlin we'll get you into another convoy to come back. We'll leave the communications truck in Berlin and you'll both come back in the jeep."

Savery was very happy about this trip; he had wondered what it was like past the death strip and he had often wondered about Berlin and the Berlin Wall. Was it like the border here? Did the West Berliners feel like prisoners? And he was also happy to be away from Grasleben and Willi the Bag, who definitely was not his old friend Rich in Monterey.

At eight the next morning the sergeants were at Checkpoint Alpha at a brief orientation. "For those of you," a lieutenant was saying, "who have never made this trip before there's nothing to worry about. Everything has been done, everyone's been notified; we just have to drive along the thruway to Berlin. Lieutenant Baxter will be in the first vehicle and I'll be in the last vehicle; we've made this trip a hundred times. There's no danger; just drive and stay in line. If your vehicle breaks down, the tow truck will take care of it. Any questions?"

Soon they were driving through the Allied checkpoint toward Marienborn, where they pulled over to the side and stopped for the Russian checkpoint, just 600 meters from where they had started. After about one hour the paperwork was done and their convoy started East again. Savery noticed that there were hundreds of cars, waiting to be processed by the East German/Soviet officials and that some must have been waiting for hours. The Autobahn was in very poor condition and the convoy proceeded slowly. Soon they encountered the first exit: Marienborn. It appeared as though any vehicle could exit there but up the exit ramp a hundred meters there was a Soviet truck parked to make certain no one did exit and so it was at every exit.

During the entire trip Savery did not see a single East German car on the Autobahn. He did notice that every house in every village they saw seemed to have one color: gray. After an uneventful three hour drive, the convoy reached the East German inspection station entering Berlin: Drewitz. After another long delay they reentered the highway for the brief one kilometer long trip to Dreilingen and the Allied Checkpoint Bravo in West Berlin. Along each side on this last section was the same tower, barbed wire fence and death strip configuration that Savery had so often seen in Helmstedt. He also noted that there was an actual wall at least 10-feet high. In a modern rest area in West Berlin just beyond the checkpoint, the convoy stopped, celebrated the successful journey and had a great US style lunch. Both Bush and Savery had scrambled eggs with bacon and toast. They already liked Berlin!

They then progressed five kilometers into the city, where they ended their journey at a huge military truck depot and were then transported by bus to a military housing unit, where they were assigned rooms for their stay. Next came the first of many orientations, lectures and films. Finally late in the afternoon after this first orientation, they were all taken to see the Friedrichstrasse border crossing into East Berlin, known as Checkpoint Charlie. It was an impressive and sobering site. The wall stretched south out of the center of town to the crossing point and took a ninety degree turn to the east for 50 meters paralleling Friedrichstrasse. It started again on the south side of Friedrichstrasse, came back west 50 meters and then turned 90 degrees to the south and continued out of sight. At the point, where the indented wall ended was the East German checkpoint only one lane wide and armed by Soviet and East German soldiers. On both sides of Friedrichstrasse behind the wall were high guard towers, just like in Helmstedt but here the soldiers were so close that Savery could see the expressions on their faces. The wall itself was at least ten feet high and had a round cement cap balanced on its top. The Allied checkpoint was in the middle of Friedrichstrasse some five meters in front of the start of the indented section of wall and was manned by US military personnel. Printed on a huge sign was a warning in Russian, German, and English. In English it read: "WARNING, YOU ARE LEAVING THE AMERICAN SECTOR!" One main difference between the two sides was that no civilians could be seen on the eastern side, while the western side was swarming with tourists. The area was full of street vendors and Savery bought a Humpelmann, a wooden figurine, painted with a Lederhosen/beer-drinking motif. It was designed to hang from a mirror. By pulling the strings attached to the arms and legs the figurine would seem to jump up into the air. Savery and Bush walking up on an observation deck to view behind the wall. They found themselves staring directly into the eyes of Soviet guards. After the initial viewing, the group was taken into some kind of a military building for a question/answer period.

"How do the East Germans maintain the wall?" came the first question.

"Actually the first six feet on this side of the wall are in East Berlin. Every now and then an armed military work crew comes out to repair the wall or to paint over the graffiti. They hate the graffiti; it's all political graffiti, anti-Wall, anti-Soviet, anti-East German."

"Why are the work crews armed? To protect themselves?

"Officially yes, but in reality they are making sure that none of them try to escape to the West."

"How long is the wall, is it just downtown?"

"No, and we are a long way from the center of town, two kilometers from the Brandenburg Gate. Actually the Berlin Wall goes entirely around West Berlin. It's longer than one hundred miles!"

"How come there are so few cars crossing here?"

"Because the crossing is for diplomats only. No West Berliner or West German can cross here. Foreigners must cross here and then only through an underground crossing below the street, the only subway crossing between the sectors."

"How many crossings are there?

"There are thirteen in all but this one gets the publicity. Most of the others are for West Berliners and/or West Germans only."

The meeting ended with the projection of a huge map of West Berlin.

During the next two days the soldiers attended many mandatory lectures and outings. They saw a video about the West Berlin mayor, Willi Brandt. They visited the Brandenburg Gate and the three airports: Gatow, run by the French, Tegel, run by the British, and Tempelhof, run by the US. At Tempelhof they watched a presentation about the 1948 Berlin Airlift, where Savery first heard the expression Rosinenbomber or Raisin bombers.

Later that day they received word that they would be joining a convoy the following morning for the drive back to Helmstedt. At 0800 they were at the meeting point and the two decided that Bush would drive the jeep and Savery would be the passenger. Savery hung his Humpelmann on the jeep's mirror. Along the way they conversed about their brief stay. They were both impressed by the positive, defiant attitude of the West Berliners, who didn't act like prisoners at all but rather liked annoyed free people.

Three hours later they arrived at the East German checkpoint in Marienborn and after a long seemingly meaningless delay were allowed to drive on into West Germany. Just twenty meters after the final inspection station the Autobahn was torn up and reconfigured into a series of sharp S-turns, apparently to prevent vehicles from racing through to the West. From the travelers point of view there was a four meter high wall which forced the traffic to take as sharp right turn and then immediately take a sharp left around another barrier and then another sharp right before one was instantaneously in West Germany. As the jeep rounded the second barrier, the sergeants were surprised to see two heavily armed Soviet guards standing shoulder to shoulder alongside the road. They were holding their machine guns at the ready and staring stern faced at the vehicles. As they got within two meters, Savery reached for the strings of his Humpelmann and pulled. Its arms and legs flew up. Instantaneously the Soviet guards burst out with a laugh. But suddenly realizing that they were laughing, they immediately returned to their menacing stare. Just think, thought Sergeant Savery, two US soldiers and two Soviet soldiers were for a very brief couple of seconds staring at each other from a distance of two meters and grinning. Savery realized again that it was just a game. The convoy stopped at the rest area and had lunch, after which Bush and Savery left the convoy and headed for Bahrdorf.

To their surprise and disappointment no one at Bahrdorf had even really noticed that they had been away. There was the normal limited intelligence activity going on but there was a new topic of conversation on everyone's lips: Willi the Bag.

It went something like this. On the day the Bush and Savery had left for Berlin, Willi had gone to Koenigslutter and got drunk with his Brit friends. A couple of them then took a train over to Hannover to a brothel and got really loaded. They wandered back into the train station where Willi got separated and went to the wrong track for the return trip, where he mistakenly got onto an express train for Hamburg.

After about twenty kilometers a conductor asked him for his ticket. He said he did not yet have one and asked for a one way ticket to Helmstedt. He became enraged when he found that he was on the wrong train and raced off toward the front of the train. Eventually he got to the front car just as the train was pulling out of Soltau. Somehow Willi managed to get into the locomotive, where he immediately threw the two drivers off the train. During the next fifteen minutes there was chaos on the racing train but two conductors eventually managed to get into the locomotive and overpower Willi and stop the train. Willi had been arrested and taken into custody by German police. There followed a two day battle between the West German federal authorities and the US military as to who had authority over Willi. The battle was even fought out in the German newspaper, die Zeit. The US military gained custody, after promising to have Willi spend years in jail.

The day before Bush and Savery had returned to Bahrdorf, Rich Williams, alias Willi the Bag, had arrived under heavy guard to Grasleben. He was handcuffed to his bed and was always, twenty-four hours a day, guarded by at least two MP's. He could not even go to the bathroom or take a shower without being handcuffed to an MP. The military was going to make an example of him.

Savery was anxious to see his old friend, to get his side of the story and so it was when they finally got back together in Grasleben.

"I've got an ace in the hole," said Rich.

"What's that? You did steal the train, didn't you?"

"Of course; it was fun!"

"What's your ace? It seems to me you're in deep shit."

"Do you remember, Bill, back in Monterey I always had an out?"

"Yes, but we never did anything like steal a train!"

"I have an out here but no one has even noticed it."

"What is it?"

"My enlistment is up tomorrow. If the military does not notice by then, they'll have to discharge me and let me go home! They'll certainly not hand me over to the Germans! I'll be a free man again!"

Rich was correct and the following day Rich was discharged and given a plane ride back to the States. It took a couple of days before anyone realized what had happened and Rich was undoubtedly off to new adventures.

VII

A week passed and the talk was still about Willi's endless episodes. There were many, many stories which Savery heard for the first time. Rich had certainly become a totally different person than he was in Monterey and Sergeant Savery found himself wondering what Rich was up to now, wherever he was.

One day Captain Baer showed up and had a meeting with the troops. Soon, very soon, Bahrdorf would permanently close and all of the remaining soldiers would work at the site near Schöningen. Most of the fifty soldiers now stationed there were living in a hotel near the center of the town. Transfers from Bahrdorf could live in the hotel or, if they preferred, could continue to live in Grasleben. Rich Williams was not even mentioned. Savery secretly and immediately decided that he wanted out of Grasleben. Except for Bush, with whom he had just become close, he had had only one real friend here, Rich Williams, and he was gone and Savery didn't like the lack of privacy, he didn't like the lack of eating possibilities, he didn't like the isolation and he didn't like the "Haifisch" or the concept of getting drunk all the time and he hoped that there would be room for him at the hotel. He was careful not to mention this to others because if they felt the same way, he might lose his opportunity in Schöningen to improve his situation. He remembered how he had heard when arriving here in Bahrdorf that Grasleben was the preferred lodging over the "Spargel" and now he was just hoping to escape. What was he getting into?

The very next day Savery was not on duty and he decided to go to Schöningen and check it out. He got a ride into Helmstedt and then followed the signs to the train station. It was bigger than he had noticed before. There were four platforms, only two of which seemed to be used, indicating a previously more active situation. Now Helmstedt was just a small place on the border and if not for the Berlin Corridor it would probably have just one active platform.

Savery bought a ticket for Schöningen for one Mark twenty and crossed under the tracks to track four. As he was coming up the stairs, he became aware that the train, hardly bigger than two busses, was just leaving. He hurried after the train and saw the conductor looking at him. For some reason he thought the conductor was encouraging him to just jump through the open door into the train. The train went faster and faster and Savery ran faster and faster. At the last second and just before the platform ended running at full speed, Savery reached into the open door, grabbed the hand rail and swung himself onto the train. In shock the conductor engaged the emergency stop and the train came to a screeching halt. Savery went sprawling on the floor, then got up and just acted like nothing had happened. He handed his ticket to the conductor, who took it and motioned for Savery to take a seat. He said only, "Soldat, ja?"

For the entire fifteen kilometers Savery just stared straight ahead but he was aware of the three old lady passengers continuously staring at him for the entire trip. Savery vowed to himself not to do this again. In Schöningen the train station was even smaller than Helmstedt but somehow had a certain charm. Following the only exit, the sergeant walked toward the center of town. It was a much bigger place than St. Andreasberg and seemed to have several thousands of inhabitants. The center was a big square where four different streets came together. Savery walked along a street leading West up the hill from the square and found a large house with a park behind it. It had a sign which read "Schützenhaus" "He actually found the hotel where the soldiers were staying but did not go in. This was definitely the correct hotel. There was loud music coming from the doorway and there were many VWs with US military plates parked outside. Savery had a sausage with french fries for lunch at a restaurant on the square. He loved the mayonnaise which came with the fries. After wandering aimlessly around for two hours, he returned to the train station, where he bought a return ticket to Helmstedt and waited for the train. The conductor was the same person as before and the sergeant was happy that the three elderly ladies were not on board. In Helmstedt he found his way to the "Haifisch," where he had a beer with some MPs from Grasleben, then got a ride back to the bomb factory.

Two weeks later the site at Bahrdorf closed. Savery got a room at the hotel and soon moved all his gear to Schöningen. The hotel, named "Zur Waldruhe" or "Forest Peace," was the only hotel in town and was chuck full of US soldiers, all working at the one site. It had forty single rooms on the second, third and fourth floors with two baths and two showers in the hall on each floor. On the first floor were quarters for the owners and a huge Gasthaus. Here the soldiers ordered and ate their meals, socialized with local girls, played music on the juke box and complained about the army while really enjoying the good life.

The owners were a young married couple Claudia and Peter. Claudia was about thirty five years old. In the last month of the war her parents were both killed in a bombing raid. They had left Claudia at home in the hotel with her brother and had gone to an aunt's house in the neighboring town of Hötensleben. After the bombing raid had subsided, her brother had raced to Hötensleben to see if his parents were OK. But another raid occurred and he was killed too. She was left alone and at the young age of fifteen inherited the entire hotel. Of course she knew nothing about running a hotel and it remained closed, slowly falling into decay for years, until Peter arrived. Peter was a British soldier, who showed up around 1955. Somehow he met Claudia and after a very short courtship, they got married. In the meantime Peter had become a German citizen and they had reopened the hotel. Shortly thereafter the US military showed up and entered an agreement to house troops in the five kilometer zone. They were really nice people and seemed to be still totally in love with each other. Claudia spoke English with a British accent. They were great cooks and served food from early morning to late evening. On the day sergeant Savery arrived, they had a "Reh", a small wild deer, dressed and hanging outside the hotel curing on a rack. Venison for supper was the overwhelming topic of the day. There were a couple soldiers there whom Savery knew but for the most part he knew no one.

During his first evening there, Savery sat in the Gasthaus and drank beer. Just like the "Stern" in Kassel the place was swarming with young, very pretty and friendly teenage girls. Savery had his dictionary and tried to speak more and more German. He sat with a soldier he knew and he introduced him to several girls. It was a pleasant evening and Savery was proud of his German ability. Something seemed to be clicking and he was understanding more and more.

The next morning all new transfers from Bahrdorf were gathered at the site in the Elm forest for an orientation. There were four shifts: one working days, one working "swings" or evenings, one working "mids" or nights, and one off on break. When on duty one had to be at the site, when off duty one could be anywhere. There were no restrictions.

The site consisted of one big one story building with several portable trailers attached around the perimeter. In the main room there were ten receivers set up to receive and record voice transmissions in the normal Soviet military frequency range. There were three more receiving stations designed to search for transmissions outside the normal range. There were stations designed to intercept Russian

Morse code. Each Morse code station was manned by a soldier who typed out the Morse code live as it came in. There were manned radar scopes. Every receiving station operator could record any transmission he encountered. It was pointed out that the Soviets had many ways to disguise their transmissions but that all of them could be immediately deciphered here. As the group was hearing this, a garbled Soviet signal was being received. The operator, a .1, merely flipped a switch and the signal was in normal Russian. The US was years ahead of the Soviets in intelligence gathering and they had no idea. One trailer contained the encoded teletype, the most important part of the entire operation. If a crisis occurred, the operator of this machine could send an emergency transmission called a critic all the way to the President of the United States if necessary. This station was manned 24 hours a day. Another trailer contained four .3 transcription stations for Russian and German. There was a maintenance trailer and a latrine. Outside there was a guard trailer and a radar tower, rising just above tree level. Around the entire site was a high barbed wire fence with one entry gate, manned by an MP. In all, twenty five persons could actively work at the site at any time if necessary. Savery noted how much bigger this site was than Bahrdorf, where only six soldiers worked at any given time.

After seeing the operations, the transfers were taken outside to a small clearing in the forest with a view to the East. Below the site was the city of Schöningen but farther East less than one kilometer was another West German town named Offleben. To the North East was still another West German town, Büddenstedt. One could clearly see the border with its death strip stretching North South across the panorama. Just beyond the death strip were the East German towns of Hötensleben and Ohrsleben. Way off in the distance were many very small East German towns. What a view! It was like looking into the living rooms of the East Germans. The transfers were told that the view of East German villages at night was very interesting and worth seeing.

Savery was assigned to the shift presently working days as a .3 transcribing Russian military transmissions. There was a second soldier named Sergeant Frank Doyle working with him. There was much more Soviet radio activity here than in Bahrdorf indicating that they were much closer. In fact the Russians often mentioned names of East German towns in their transmissions and most were just over the border. Savery enjoyed working this shift and got along well with everyone. In one trailer there was a map of the immediate East German sector and Savery looked at the map every time he heard a town mentioned. It was exciting for him to imagine what was going on just over the border and he imagined seeing Russian soldiers scurrying about. Every shift brought a new challenge to keep up with the high volume of material which needed transcription. Sergeant Doyle's understanding of Russian was very good and the two soldiers often worked together on difficult material.

One day Doyle and Savery got into a conversation.

"You seem different than the average soldier here," he said.

"What do you mean?" asked Savery.

"I've noticed that you aren't out after every girl for one thing," said Doyle.

"I'm enjoying life, I like talking with all of them. Why?"

"I have a girlfriend here and I'm planning to marry her."

"Congratulations," said Savery, realizing that he had not noticed Doyle chatting with girls in the hotel.

"Her name is Dora and she has a good friend, Ilse."

"Yes," said Savery. "What do you have in mind?"

"I thought you might like to double date. I've already asked Dora and Ilse and they're for it. I've told them that you seem to be an OK guy."

"That seems great. Do they speak English?" asked Savery.

"Some, but not as much as the girls in the hotel," said Doyle.

"When do you have in mind and what will we do?" asked Savery.

"We are both off Saturday. How does that sound, Saturday night? We'll take my VW and go out to dinner and then just look for something to do."

"That sounds great," responded Savery. "I'll bring my dictionary!"

Sergeant Savery spent the next couple nights practicing his German with girls in the hotel. His dictionary got a lot of work.

Saturday night finally arrived. Doyle walked into the hotel with the two girls, where they were introduced to Savery. Dora was good-looking but Ilse was beautiful.

"Bill, that's a nice name," said Ilse with a strong German accent. They decided to drive into Helmstedt to eat at the "Haifisch" but the girls did not like it there and after some indecision they ended up back in Bahrdorf at the "Spargel" where Frank had also once lived. Horst and Gabriela were very friendly. There were a lot of guests in the Gasthaus, eating, drinking, playing music on the jukebox, and even dancing. Nina was there. She came over to Sergeant Savery as he was putting coins into the juke box; they talked for a couple minutes and then she left. One could see that she was not happy to see Savery with another, younger girl. The four of them enjoyed their meal and were engaged in a lively conversation, when all of a sudden there was a long silence. Savery wanted to ask Ilse if she were bored. He hurriedly looked in his dictionary . . . to bore, to bore . . . and then he asked her, "Bohren Sie?" She answered, "Ja, in die Nase!" while sticking her pointer finger into her nose. The three of them burst out laughing. Savery had no idea what was so funny but he was convinced he had somehow made a great joke. And so it went, light hearted and happy for almost an hour.

It was decided to continue the night's activity in another place. Someone came up with idea of driving all the way to Hannover to visit some bars Frank had heard about and so about 10 p.m. they arrived in Hannover and hopped from bar to bar in the red light section of town.

Eventually they were sitting in a bar laughing, drinking and talking with each other. For some reason Savery noticed that Ilse and Dora were the only girls in the place, when all of a sudden five very pretty girls walked in. Everyone knew them from the bartenders to the clientele. After fifteen minutes one of the girls took an apparent interest in Sergeant Savery. She came over to the two couples and introduced herself as Lola but really directed her conversation toward Sergeant Savery. She came back with a liter glass of beer for him, even though he told her that he did not want it. She came over a third time just to say a few words to him. After the third time, Frank said, "Does anyone notice anything strange about this bar?" No one did.

"These girls are prostitutes. They must have just got off work and these men here are their pimps." The three looked around; Frank was correct. Just then the same girl approached them again, but this time she drew up a chair and squeezed in next to Savery. Lola obviously did not like Ilse because she was with Savery. She just ignored the others at the table and talked to Savery, continually saying sweet things to him while getting as close to him as she could. At one point she put her hand on Savery's thigh and glared at Ilse.

"I'll give you a great time. I'll fulfill all your fantasies; just spend the night with me," she whispered in his ear. Savery noticed that he was instantaneously aroused.

Savery had never been in a situation like this. He had come with Ilse and was having a fun evening with her until now but, on the other hand, Lola was very pretty and very young and he longed to discover her secrets and he was drunk and enjoying the moment. After about ten more minutes Lola said to him, "It's time to make up your mind. Everything I have is yours. Let's go now upstairs to my room!"

Savery weighed the situation and in the end decided to remain with Ilse. He could see himself in a longer more meaningful relationship with her.

"I'll stay with her," he told Lola as he glanced smilingly toward Ilse.

When Lola realized that she had been rejected, she instantly became extremely jealous and enraged, stood up and spit in Savery's face. Ilse hopped up from her seat and pushed Lola away and instantaneously the entire clientele started to yell, push and fight. Somehow the four of them escaped without being injured and ran down a side street to their parked car.

The ride home along the Autobahn took more than an hour. They all laughed and retold the events from their own perspectives. Ilse and Savery sat in the back. Frank dropped the girls off on some street in Schöningen. Savery did not even get to kiss Ilse because someone inside the building, probably her mother, turned her outside light on.

The next day Savery got out this dictionary to see what he had done wrong the night before. He had wanted to say "Are you bored?" But he found "to bore" or to drill a hole. He had asked Isle if she were drilling a hole, not if she were bored. She had answered yes, in her nose and had pretended to drill her finger into her nose. It was funny but the sergeant realized he had much more work left to speak German the way he wanted to. As for Ilse, Savery would never see her again, but he would remember Lola for a very long time. It was a memorable evening.

A few days later Sergeant Savery was working mids, when a Russian .2 called him over to his receiver and handed him his head phones.

"Listen to this," he said. "It sounds like Russian but I cannot understand it."

Savery put of his head phones and listened. He instantaneously recognized it as Russian and also as the same type transmission he had heard in Bahrdorf, except here it was coming in much clearer. "Are you recording this?" Savery asked.

"Of course, but I missed the beginning" responded the .2. After listening for a moment, Savery called the other .3, Doyle, from his trailer and soon all three of them were listening to the live transmission. As was the case before, the transmission was often over modulated and often faded out but it was much more understandable. They agreed that it was not a military transmission but was about the military. Doyle and Savery decided to work on it together and send it down to headquarters. After the transmission ended, they took the tape into their trailer and both listened to the entire recording from the beginning. They then worked on it together, transcribing word for word everything that was understandable. The entire transmission amounted to two typed pages in Russian. They then teletyped it down to Kassel. Both soldiers were impressed by the other's knowledge of Russian. Doyle thought he would be much better, having been on the job for so long, and Savery thought he would be much better, having had so much more language training. As it turned out, they were both very pleased by their accomplishment and by the way they worked together. They both wondered what headquarters and Burt Nelson would think about it.

Five days later they got their answer, when they received a package addressed to them from Burt Nelson. When they opened the package, there was just the last Sunday's edition of the Russian newspaper "Izvestia," published in Moscow; that was all, no explanation. They leafed through the newspaper together and found, much to their surprise, their entire transmission, starting with a couple sentences that had not been recorded by their .2. It turned out to be a new feature of "Izvestia," a weekly article about the Vietnam War. This was sent weekly by normal voice transmission from Hanoi to Moscow and it turned out that there was a straight line from Hanoi through Moscow to Schöningen and by skips in the atmosphere it was generally clear even in Schöningen.

Later in the day Burt Nelson called them on the encoded line, congratulated them, and told them, that, even though there was nothing of any intelligence value in the transmissions, he would like Savery and Doyle to transcribe each weekly article if they continued to be readable. When asked if he also wanted them translated into English, Nelson said no, they could handle that. And so for the next several months, Doyle and Savery provided the US military with the "Izvestia" article several hours before the Russians got the same information.

Word of this development spread quickly around the site and all were proud of their accomplishments. Even the brass at Intelligence Headquarters Europe informed the site of their pleasure.

VIII

A week later on day shift Sergeant Savery was transcribing a long conversation concerning a Soviet artillery company, when the conversation suddenly switched into German. Not knowing enough technical German to accurately continue, Savery went over to a German .3 to get some help. Sergeant Frederick came over to Savery's station, sat down, and in fifteen minutes transcribed the German part of the conversation. When he ended, Savery asked him, "Who are you?"

"I'm Sergeant Frederick, Mike Frederick. You know me."

"Yes, I know, but who are you?"

"I don't understand. What do you mean?"

"It just occurred to me that I see you only here at the site. I've never seen you off duty. I've never even seen you at the hotel."

"Because I don't live at the hotel. A lot of us don't live there."

"You don't live there? Where DO you live?"

"I have a private room."

"You have a private room? Can you do that?

"Sure, anyone can do that. You can do that."

"I can do that? How?"

"By putting an advertisement in the paper. Do you want me to put an ad in for you?"

"Is the military OK with that?"

"Sure, why not? Do you want me to put in an ad or not?"

"How much does a private room cost?"

"Cheaper than the hotel, around 100 Marks a month, $25."

"Is that all?" asked Savery flabbergasted. "Where do you eat?"

"I eat mostly at the hotel but I only go there to eat. Most of my friends are German and I hang out with them. I AM a German .3 after all."

"How long will it take to find a place?"

"The weekly paper comes out on Saturdays. If I put in the ad on time, it will be in the paper this Saturday. I'll use my address for any response and we should hear something in about a week from now, OK?"

"OK, let's do it. I don't like sitting in the hotel all the time and I'm looking for something new."

"Are you sure, you want to do it? I don't want you to back out."

"I won't. Place the ad!" responded Savery.

All week Savery thought about a private room. He decided that he needed another car, one to actually drive around with and not to crash and he actually found a soldier, who was just about to be discharged and he agreed to buy his VW Beetle, his fourth car, for 100 Marks or $25. They signed the transfer of ownership and took all the paperwork to the PX in Helmstedt. He wondered what else he would need; he already had toiletries and towels. He would definitely need an alarm clock. Savery bought a copy of the Saturday Schöningener Wochendliche Zeitung and their ad was in it. It stated: "Amer. Soldat sucht Privatzimmer in Schöningen. Bitte Möglichkeiten an Frederick, Elmstrasse 21, Schöningen zu schicken." Savery noted that the newspaper was only six pages long. The front page had a big picture of some high school event. In the bottom-right corner was written in small letters "püppe" and he theorized that that was the photographer.

The following Thursday Sergeant Frederick showed up at the site with two responses. One concerned a room at a house in Esbeck, a town a kilometer toward Helmstedt. "Too far out of town," said Frederick and tossed the letter in a trash bag. The other offered two different private rooms for two soldiers and was only three blocks from the hotel. The letter read: "Zwei private Dachzimmer an zwei Soldaten zu vermieten. 100 Mark pro Zimmer pro Monat. Bitte wenden an Frau Lange, Ostendorfstrasse 24. Telefonnummer 20 30 44."

"What do you think, Savery? Do you want to take a look?"

"Two rooms?"

"No problem, Corporal Jim Carocci, a German .2, is also looking for a room. We could invite him along," said Frederick.

"I've met him, seems like an OK guy," said Savery.

"I'll call her and set up a meeting, how about tomorrow afternoon?"

"Agreed!" said Savery.

"At five to six the next afternoon the three soldiers left the hotel for the three-minute walk to Ostendorfstrasse 24. They rang the doorbell and an old lady met them and led them into a hallway, then up the stairs to the second floor, where she stopped and rapped on a door. An old man came out and the Lady said in German: "Ich bin Frau Lange; das ist mein Mann, Willi." We introduced ourselves. Frederick exchanged a few words with them and told them that Jim Carocci and Bill Savery were interested in renting the rooms. Frau Lange shook hands with each and tried to call them by their first names, which Savery thought was very friendly. Frau Lange, who spoke not one word of English, stated that a family rented the first floor, that she and her husband lived on the second floor and that the rooms to be rented were on the third floor, just under the roof. She then led the way to the third floor, her husband taking up the rear.

The third floor had five closed doors, two on each side and one at the front end of the hallway. She went to that door and opened it. It was the bath with a sink, a toilette, and a shower. The bathroom was basic but pleasant and appeared to have been recently remodeled.

After the soldiers had nodded their approval, Frau Lange unlocked and opened the room to the left of the bath. It was a spacious room of about fifteen by twelve feet and also appeared to have been recently remodeled. The front of the room had a slanted ceiling, which came down to two feet from the floor. There was therefore no window but in the ceiling there was a skylight window which allowed in much light and which also could be opened. Herr Lange opened and closed this window several times to reassure them of its functionality. Savery actually pulled up a chair, stood on it, and looked out the skylight onto the rooftops of buildings across the street. Herr Lange was not happy with Savery doing this and indicated for him to get down.

The room had a single bed, a small table, three wooden chairs, two lamps, a German style dresser, some shelves and a sink. There were even four pictures on the side wall. The sink had only cold water. Carocci noticed this and asked about it but was told that the sink in the bath had hot water.

There were also four electrical wall outlets. The actual wiring ran outside the walls and was stapled to the wall. This was especially noticeable near the door, where the wires exposed from the floor to the ceiling.

After looking around and asking a few questions, the soldiers were led into the room to the right of the bathroom. It was a mirror image of the first room. Savery liked the first room better for some reason and the two agreed by nods to take the rooms. Back out in the hallway Frau Lange told them, that the rent was 100 Marks a month payable in advance on the first of each month, that they each would get a key to the front entry way and to his room.

After a private conversation between the three of them, the soldiers decided to rent the rooms. They all agreed that although very friendly, both Frau Lange and her husband, Willi, seemed a little strange, probably because they were older or because Carocci and Savery were American soldiers. They each paid the 100 Marks, got their keys and left for the day. Very happy, they returned to the hotel and had a great German meal of Schnitzel, Rotkohl and Pommes Frites with Mayonnaise.

Within a couple days they had carried their personal gear to Ostendorfstrasse 24 and checked out of the hotel. Peter was OK with it and wished them well, saying he hoped they would continue to eat meals in the hotel and to come and enjoy the nightlife. Their first night in their new private rooms was uneventful. They had walked there together after their day shift, had changed their uniforms for civilian clothing and had gone back to the hotel to eat and socialize. About dark they had gone back, used a key on the outside door and had heard a door closing in the back of the first floor as they climbed the stairs to the third floor. They actually kept their doors open for a while so that they could talk to each other. Finally after closing his door, Savery could occasionally hear doors opening and closing and could hear an occasional voice from down below and he wondered who lived on the first floor. Were they old people like Frau Lange and her husband Willi?

The following morning both soldiers overslept and after taking showers rushed down the stairs together. They decided that they had better call quickly to the hotel to try to get a ride to the site. They rapped on Frau Lange's door and she opened up.

"Telefon, Telefon, bitte," said Carocci.

"Kein Telefon, nix Telefon" answered Frau Lange. "Unten ist Telefon." They continued down to the first floor and rapped on a door near the front of the building. They rapped a second time and the door opened. The lady, who opened the door, said: "Bitte?"

"Telefon, bitte," said Carocci.

"Kein Telefon."

"Bitte!" repeated Carocci. "Frau Lange hat gesagt, hier ist Telefon. Wir muessen telefonieren."

"Bitte!" said the lady hesitantly and let the soldiers enter the room. She pointed to the phone and Carocchi dialed the hotel number, spoke with Peter and then with some soldier, who promised to wait for them at the hotel. This took a couple minutes and Savery used the time to look around the room and to meet the lady. He pointed to himself and said "Bill." The lady pointed to herself and said "Frau Schünemann." After the phone call the soldiers thanked the lady and rushed away to the hotel.

Work dragged by all day because they had not eaten any breakfast. Everyone wanted to know how the first night had gone but there was nothing of interest to report. In the night another Vietnam War report for "Izvestia" had been recorded and Savery spent two hours transcribing it and sending it to headquarters. After work they got a ride back to the hotel, where they did not even go home to change but, instead, both ordered big meals and beer. Savery walked to Ostendorfstrasse before Carocci, and, when he opened the front door, a teenage girl was just crossing the central hallway in the rear of the house. She said "Guten Tag!" just before exiting out of sight through a door. Savery did not get a good look at her but he realized that there must be a real family living there.

The next morning Carocci wanted to use the phone again and so the two of them rapped on the door again and again the same lady opened up and let them use the phone. Savery repeated his name as "Bill" and the lady did the same as "Frau Schünemann." This time Savery noticed many family pictures on the walls, overstuffed sofas and chairs and a piano. He also noticed a second room in the back. It seemed to him that the lady was genuinely friendly. Carocci just noticed the phone call and was surprised that Savery saw so much.

After work that afternoon the two soldiers decided to go out into the back courtyard. They still had their uniform fatigues on and were sitting at a small table, when Frau Schünemann and two girls came out. Frau Schuenemann introduced the two girls.

"Das sind meine Töchter, Juliane und Christine."

"Bill," said Savery and extended his hand to the girls.

"Jim," said Carocci, and did the same.

"Ich heisse Christine, I speak English, you can speak English."

"No," said Bill. "I want to learn German. Can we speak German?"

"Our mother and father know no English."

"That settles it; I will try to speak German and I have a small dictionary right here," and he took out his dictionary.

The conversation immediately turned to German and, in fact, except for an occasional word, Savery's entire relationship with the Schünemann family would be exclusively in German. For Jim this switch to German would be very easy, being trained as a German .2. At some point during this brief initial encounter Jim ran up to his room and brought down his helmet. The girls were trying it on, when their father came home and entered the back yard. He was obviously upset and simply said "Lass das!" or "Quit it!" and went back into the house. Savery realized that something was wrong and the conversation broke off.

During the next week the four of them met several times in the courtyard, during which time the mother was always present. The four got along well and actually played a game of cards together and tried to play chess. The father was never there. Juliane was seventeen years old and attended the local high school. She did not really like school and wanted to become a store window decorator. Christine was three years older, had finished high school and was doing an apprenticeship at the local newspaper as a reporter/photographer. Her pictures in the paper always had the designation "püppe." Neither girl had ever met an American much less an American soldier and they were curious to learn more. They had always been forbidden by the father to go to the hotel and now that they had soldiers living in their building. Their mother wanted to be sure that their acquaintance would be proper. That is why she brought them into the courtyard when Jim and Bill were there. The father was not convinced that any contact was proper and stayed, for the most part, separated from the situation. He seemed to take a two hour walk most every afternoon.

In any event both girls seemed well adjusted and not the type of girls that were always in the hotel. Savery immediately liked the older sister, Christine. She was only a year younger then he, and seemed to see the world as he did. She was very pretty, had long light brown hair which she kept in pig tails, brown eyes and was one inch shorter than he. She, in turn, seemed to like Bill and often directed her remarks to him, or so Bill thought. There was, on the other hand, never any hint of improper behavior. They just seemed to get along well.

Jim preferred Juliane for the same reasons. She was taller, had dark brown hair and brown eyes and wore glasses. Both were taller than their parents. Frau Schünemann was in her forties and seemed to be trying to hold on to her youth. Part of that was undoubtedly monitoring the relationships of her kids. Herr Schünemann, in his late forties, seemed to be in poor health and, judging by his schedule, did not appear to have a job. Savery wondered what was in his past. Had he been a soldier too, had he been a Nazi, had he fought against the Americans, had he been in Russia? Probably not in Russia because very few of those soldiers ever returned to Germany and he did not seem to be the Nazi type, whatever that was. For some reason, perhaps the way his kids had been brought up, perhaps the affectionate way his girls talked about him, Savery did not feel Herr Schünemann had been a Nazi.

Juliane and Christine referred to their parents as "Vati" and "Mutti" and by the end of that week the soldiers were addressing Frau Schünemann as "Mutti." She seemed to be flattered and allowed them to continue. They decided to continue to address her husband as Herr Schünemann; they had not seen him as often, had not really conversed with him and did not want to offend him.

On Saturday night the Schünemanns invited the soldiers to Sunday afternoon coffee and pastry, Frau Schünemann's personal cheese cake.

The entire family was there and Christine played a song on the piano. She apologized that she did not play better but both soldiers were impressed. Herr Schünemann was friendly but aloof; he seemed to be still assessing the soldiers.

Frau Lange and her husband Willi were always scurrying around the house and seemed to be always watching. It seemed that, for some reason, they did not approve of the growing relationship between the soldiers and the downstairs tenants.

For some reason the paperwork for the car took forever but finally the plates came and Sergeant Savery could drive his car, his fourth Beetle. He loved the Elm forest and drove through it from several directions. It actually stretched from Schöningen westward some forty five kilometers to Braunschweig. Nestled around the fringes were many little villages with cool names like Schöppenstedt and Langeleben and Savery wanted to experience them all. Of course Königslutter was right in the middle. One day he parked his car near a walking path and walked out into the forest a few hundred meters. He stopped and was staring out into the trees, when he saw some movement. He remained motionless and silent for about five minutes when a wild boar appeared in the distance. Soon more and more wild boars appeared until there were about twenty five. Each pig was the size of an average domestic pig but was black and had tusks. They either didn't see that there was a human close by or didn't care but after a few minutes they continued their foraging out of site. Savery told Herr Schünemann about this and for the first time he opened up and really talked to Savery, telling him that wild boars were very dangerous and not to be taken lightly, because they often attacked humans. Savery liked talking with him. He seemed calm and understanding and he called Sergeant Savery simply Bill like the rest of his family.

Weeks went by and Jim and Bill, except for one three-day period, when Mutti had told Bill and Jim not to come by, spent more and more time with the Schünemanns. One day Herr Schünemann asked Savery if he wanted to go to his "Stammtisch" with him. Savery had no idea what a Stammtisch was but said OK. Savery offered him a ride there and he accepted. Along the way Herr Schuenemann said that this was the first time in two years that he had been in a car.

They drove in the direction of the Elm. Right at the edge of town they stopped at a Gasthaus called the "Schützenhaus." Before they entered, Herr Schünemann told Savery not to sit down unless all persons at the table invited him. There were five men, all in the same age group, sitting at the table: the owner of the Gasthaus, Herr Schünemann's doctor, and three of his boyhood friends. Herr Schünemann introduced the sergeant as Bill and one by one each person, after some side discussion, agreed to let him join them. Before he sat down he shook hands with each. All in all it went OK and Bill was invited back with Herr Schünemann. On the way home Herr Schünemann surprised Savery by inviting him to call him Rolf or Vati. He said it was weird to hear Bill call his wife Mutti and him Herr Schünemann. This would be more consistent. Rolf even told Bill about his extensive stamp collection. He said he had thousands of stamps which he had been collecting since his return from the war. After arriving back home, Rolf got out some of his favorite stamps and showed them to Bill. Mutti and the girls were very happy about this development.

One day Bill and Jim decided to find out what was in Ostendorf; they lived on Ostendorfstrasse and they were curious what was there. They had never met anyone from Ostendorf. They wanted to drive East out of town but the street led under the railroad tracks and abruptly ended. Everything around them, all the structures lay in ruin. Off in the distance was the town of Offleben but there seemed to be no road to get there and, in fact, the town seemed abandoned. They got out of the car and noticed that the border, the death strip, was just a few hundred meters on their right. They got an idea to wave to the East German border guards. Savery took a white towel from his car and the two soldiers walked toward the death strip, making sure not to enter it. Finally from a safe looking place they started to wave their towel. No response but they could see the guards watching them. This time they both just waved and one of the guards on the other side waved back. Later Rolf said never to do that again, that one could get killed doing that. He said Offleben had been totally abandoned after the war and now the neighboring towns of Offleben and Büddenstedt had been taken over by the West German coal industry.

Weeks went by. Things were very busy at the site because the Russians and East Germans across the border were suddenly very active. One day Captain Baer showed up and everyone was called to the site for a meeting concerning impending changes. As it turned out, two sergeants, who were each in charge of entire shifts, were being discharged so different soldiers would be taking over their positions. The new persons in charge would be Sergeant Roetter and Sergeant Savery.

Sergeant Savery was flabbergasted; he certainly did not expect to be considered for the position. A round of applause broke out for the two sergeants. Later in a private meeting Captain Baer told the two sergeants that the outgoing shift chiefs had suggested their names because they felt these were the most qualified. Each sergeant would shadow their shift chief for the next week before officially taking over.

On his very first mid shift in charge and interesting event occurred. It seemed like the usual slow night with just a few radio checks detected. At about 2 a.m. one soldier went outside to stretch and decided to walk the few meters to the clearing and look down at Schöningen. While he was there, he saw two flares go off across the border. These flares traditionally meant, that someone had accidentally tripped them, perhaps trying to escape, or that they were intentionally sent off to identify some problem. The soldier noted that these flares were a long way from the border, perhaps five kilometers. After a couple minutes another flare went up, which seemed to be closer to the border.

The soldier returned to his duty station and told Sergeant Savery what he had seen. Savery in turn, asked the soldiers at the receivers if they were hearing any unusual activity and, in fact, they were. Savery gathered the best linguists around the receivers, switched on the speakers, and listened in. They heard open transmissions in Russian and German. From the transmissions they learned that a Russian soldier had stolen a Russian military vehicle and was driving around with his German girlfriend. They appeared to be headed toward the border. The transmissions seemed to be more and more frequent, so Sergeant Savery sent two soldiers out to the clearing to just watch. What they saw was a steady stream of flares zigzagging across the panorama but getting closer and closer to the border. From the transmissions it became clear that they were headed toward the border and that the East German authorities were trying to stop them. They heard the East German border town of Hötensleben, just across the border, mentioned, signifying that the pair was quickly approaching the border. Savery told two solders to remain and keep recording and then told all others to come with him to the clearing. There were flares going off everywhere across the border, all very close. The soldiers stared in awe and the ongoing spectacle. Suddenly out of the silence and darkness came the sound of machinegun fire, followed by explosions. They had made it to the death strip. After a few moments it became silent again and the flares abruptly stopped. Within another couple minutes the radio transmissions also stopped and it turned into another normal night shift. But it was clear that they had just witnessed an attempt to escape to the West. It occurred to Savery that the same border guard who had waved to him recently in Ostendorf might have been the machine gunner who foiled the escape. By the end of the shift they had transcribed the tapes and sent them along with a general description of the events to headquarters.

Another strange occurrence happened during these weeks. Sergeant Savery came home one day to find an opened letter lying on his bed. It was a letter from home and he had received and read it the day before. He thought he had placed it under his uniforms on a shelf. He was confused but thought he had forgotten exactly what he had done with the letter. A few days later Savery was sure that his room had been rearranged. He mentioned it to Frau Lange but she made no clear answer.

In the meantime the sergeant was spending more and more time on the first floor. He started playing chess every day with Mutti. Neither knew how to play but they were becoming better every day. It got to the point where they were playing as many as ten games a day. In all these endless games Savery won every time and Mutti was very aggravated.

One day Christine, Mutti and Bill took a long walk on a hiking trail along the edge of the Elm. They ended up at a restaurant named Waldfrieden. It was a restaurant which specialized in its home made cherry wine and pastry. It was delicious and both ladies were obviously hooked on the wine. This was just one of many things they did together but it became clear that Christine and Bill were interested, first of all and foremost, in each other. They used every occasion to be together, to talk about anything together, to play cards together, to listen to music together on Christine's record player, to do anything together. Once she read in the paper that a course in Russian would be offered in the evening at the local high school. She wanted to be together with Bill and away from her parents and asked Bill if he wanted to take beginning Russian with her. Bill explained that he could not possibly pull it off. He was totally fluent in Russian and didn't know how to disguise that. But he wanted to be with her and they both signed up for the course. They were both happy that her parents were in agreement and they attended the first class. The teacher immediately recognized Savery's ability in Russian and repeatedly said to him in German: "You know Russian!" After three classes they did not attend anymore. It was embarrassing. Bill just could not fake it, no matter how much he tried. During these weeks they did not even one time have any physical contact. There was definitely a sexual attraction but first of all they were becoming best friends. Christine was the first girl he had ever met who seemed to be genuinely interested in him, in his youth, in his life, and his family in the mountains of Vermont, and who looked up to him as being very special to her. She, in turn, talked about her youth, her interests, and her hopes for the future. She loved photography, wanted to help people, become a reporter, and eventually a mother. Her parents really didn't seem to notice this growing relationship and therefore probably allowed them to continue. They seemed to think it was innocent.

Often Christine seemed somehow sad and Bill asked her several times if everything was OK and she always said all was fine and that she was very happy. Bill felt totally happy and, to him, she felt the same. But then he couldn't figure out, why she sometimes seemed sad. Her taste in music was old fashioned. She seemed to like Mitch Miller. She had several of his records and often played his albums. Her favorite song was "Willow, weep for me," and she always became sad when she played it.

Rolf became more and more friendly with Bill every day and often talked with him about everything from nature to politics. He loved the Elm and had wandered through the Elm as a child, hoping to see a "Hirsch" or white tailed deer. He had only once seen one. Politically he seemed to be a fan of Willi Brandt. The only thing Bill knew about him was that he was mayor of West Berlin.

Jim and Juliane seemed to drop off the radar. Bill never asked what they were doing together. They were just there, doing their own thing. In fact the parents did not seem to be concerned or even attentive. They seemed to be preoccupied with Christine and Bill.

One thing that the four often did together was to visit the local "Milchbar" or ice cream shop. It was just three blocks away and had great ice cream and was always full of teenagers. Everyone knew Juliane, because she was also a high school student like most of them. Christine, being older, seldom saw anyone she knew so felt at ease, visiting there with her sister, Bill and Jim. She would never go just with Bill. Juliane liked to show off Jim to her friends, making her seem somehow better.

IX

After months of emotions concerning Sergeant Savery, starting with fear, dread and apprehension and finally reaching acceptance and affection, Rolf Schünemann finally told Bill his story. One summer day he invited Bill into the back Hof, got each a beer, told his family not to interrupt and started talking in German. He explained how he had dreaded this conversation but it was now time because Bill had somehow erased his fears and restored his faith in humanity.

As a young teenager Rolf had often traveled to France, where he had French relatives. For years he had spent every long school vacation in Paris and had become totally fluent in French. His relatives had taken him to Normandy and even several times to Spain and Belgium. He developed a great love for France and the French people. When Hitler came to power, his relatives were very concerned, but, being apolitical and very young, Rolf dismissed their concerns and told them not to worry.

When Rolf turned eighteen he was drafted and eventually was trained as a forward observer in the artillery, specifically for a "Big Bertha" battalion. He was not part of the invasion of France but later was assigned to a unit in Normandy. He actually saw his relatives once when on weekend leave to Paris. They were very unappreciative and hated the Nazi occupying forces but he assured them that everything would turn out alright.

Once in 1942 he was allowed to go back to his home town on leave. His father had died and by the time Rolf arrived in Schöningen, his father had been buried. He was happy to see his wife after two years and, as it turned out, they conceived their first born, Christine. But an event was about to occur, that changed his attitude toward Hitler and made him see things in a different light.

At 8 p.m. the warning sirens blasted three times. It was a signal for the entire town, men, women, and children, to gather in the central square. By the time Rolf and his wife reached the square, thousands of people were already there. The East side of the square was lined with military trucks, parked with their backs to the square. After all the people had arrived, the streets exiting the square were blocked off so that no one could escape. After a few minutes a platform was set up behind the trucks and three SS officers in their black uniforms climbed onto the platform to address the crowd. An air of apprehension came over Rolf as he watched what was unfolding. He sensed that something bad was about to occur. One SS officer through a loudspeaker made the following statement in German. "Citizens of Schöningen, last month you were ordered to surrender your Jews. We have information that several of you are still hiding some Jews and you are to surrender them NOW to us. Is that understood?"

A murmur of dread went through the crowd.

"Surrender your Jews NOW!" repeated the SS officer through the loudspeaker. No one moved. Suddenly the tailgates of the trucks dropped open, revealing men with mounted machine guns.

A gasp went through the crowd, and people tried to escape from the square but were blocked.

One machine gun began firing into the crowd! After a thirty second burst which killed or wounded hundreds, people started yelling, "He's a Jew; these are Jews!" In all, only about twenty would-be

Jews were given up and the incident was over. The people were allowed to go back to their homes. But in that one incident, Rolf realized that everything he had heard about the Nazis was correct, everything he had denied and denied and denied. And he knew Germany would pay for this. He knew that God would not let this stand. He didn't know when or how but he knew what would come.

When his leave was over, he said goodbye to his wife and returned to Normandy. He never mentioned this incidence to French acquaintances and he never mentioned it to his fellow soldiers. He was afraid that someone might sense his attitude and then he too might have an encounter with the SS.

Two years went by and Rolf was still in Normandy. He missed his wife and longed to see his daughter, Christine. In these two years he had witnessed the construction of huge defenses along the ocean, and he knew that no one could possibly successfully land against these defenses.

When the invasion came, Rolf had done nothing for two years. He had not fired his rifle in months and it was rusty. The actual night was windy and rainy. During the night the pounding of shells was like a nightmare and as dawn approached so many ships were visible that Rolf could not see any water and he knew it was over. At first dawn all artillery forward observers were called back to a point about 2 kilometers from the beaches and this probably saved Rolf's life.

The rest of the war was one large retreat for Rolf and his unit. He retreated across northern France, through Belgium into western Germany. He was in the Battle of the Bulge, where officers in his unit wanted to surrender. Rolf saved the day and the unit did not surrender because Rolf, having been to that exact area several times with his French relatives, knew a way out. It was here that Rolf killed his first and only human being, an American soldier. "It was him or me," Rolf said as he cried.

Later Rolf's unit was one of the last to cross the bridge at Remagen. Eventually his unit retreated into Czechoslovakia, where it surrendered to American soldiers. Of fifty in his original unit only two had survived. Rolf was fearful of the Americans but also glad that the war was over and he hoped he would soon see his wife and child.

For six weeks everyone in his unit was detained and processed. Each was given an identity card, showing information such as name, prewar address, rank, and German military unit. Each was given six days' worth of military rations and was then told to walk home. Rolf was greatly relieved.

On the sixteenth day of walking he passed through St. Andreasberg. He was amazed that it did not lay in ruin and he remembered traveling there as a boy with his parents, back before the Nazis.

On the twenty second day he walked through the Elm and from a clearing he looked down at his beloved home. His heart swelled with joy as he envisioned his wife and child.

As he was staring down at his hometown, a US military jeep drove up to him, stopped, and two soldiers got out. One asked to see his ID, after which he was told to get into the jeep.

Rolf, who spoke no English, tried to resist. He told them his home was just down the hill, that his wife was waiting for him, that there was no reason for him to go with them, but they, probably understanding little or no German, could not be convinced and Rolf was driven away. The soldiers were concerned about Rolf's identification card. In the military unit box was SS and because of this he was being taken into custody.

Rolf explained to Bill that he was in the "fighting SS" a forward observer for the artillery and not the dreaded SS with their black uniforms. But Savery had long since known the difference.

Rolf was taken to an American concentration camp in Bad Kreuznach. When Savery insisted that there were no American concentration camps, Rolf answered that there had been one, that he had been in it. The camp had been set up after the war ended. When the US found the Nazi concentration camps, it decided to round up all SS troops and put them into a concentration camp too to partially get even. This camp was set up in the forest outside Bad Kreuznach and was one kilometer by one kilometer square. There were no real bathrooms, a brook ran through the camp and prisoners drank the water at one end and relieved themselves at the other end. There were also no permanent buildings so prisoners were rained on and snowed on and exposed to the weather twenty four hours a day.

There was little attempt at accurate record keeping. Some German prisoners were employed as aids to the US military personnel and they in turn tried to keep a roster of prisoners but hundreds or even thousands of soldiers died of exposure.

Rolf was in this camp from summer 1945 to spring 1946 and he probably would have died if not for one incident. In the late winter one of the prisoner aids recognized the name Rolf Schünemann on a list and he wondered if it was his old boyhood friend from Schöningen. He wandered through the camp, calling out the name Rolf Schünemann. He had just given up, when a prisoner said to him, that he thought the soldier lying in the slime ahead of them was so named. This aid fished the semi-conscious man out of the mud and it was indeed his old boyhood friend. He was nursed back to life and after a couple months started to work for the US military. Just one week later the camp was suddenly closed and the prisoners were told to walk home.

And so it came that in May 1946 Rolf Schünemann was standing at the exact same clearing in the Elm, where he was taken prisoner almost a year earlier, and was staring down at his village. He somehow expected to be taken prisoner again but he was not and he wandered down into town, his heart pounding.

His wife, upon seeing him at her door, fell unconscious on the door steps. She had thought that he was dead and had expected to never see him again.

Since that day nineteen years ago he had never talked to an American soldier. He had avoided all contact, being afraid that they would arrest him and take him from his family. Only through his contact with Bill was his faith restored. Rolf apologized for his unfriendliness in the beginning but Savery hadn't even noticed that he was unfriendly. He thought he was just being protective of his family.

But Rolf was not done with his story. In the years after his return, he had come down with a mysterious heart condition. He had got a job at the local coal plant but found work there more and more stressful and there came a time in 1955 when he had to give up his job and go on public assistance. His heart condition got worse and for the years since he was seeing a heart doctor every month. He was to avoid all stress and it seemed to him that there was only stress in his life. For years now he had been carrying around with him cyanide tablets in case he felt a heart attack coming on and a few times he had taken a cyanide tablet and then been transported to the hospital where he had recovered.

In 1959 he had run out of funds was forced to sell his house. He desperately wanted to protect his family and keep them together and had tried everything to hold on to his house. For years they had rented the 2nd floor to a family, consisting of a father, a mother and one son. They had not always got along well with this family but the money helped them for years to stay afloat. Financially things still got worse and worse. Finally there was no other recourse than to sell and their renters were more than willing to buy the house. In fact, they had been trying to buy the house for three years. Their son had a high paying job for the West German federal government, whereby he traveled to foreign countries to help arrange for guest workers, "Gastarbeiter," to come to Germany and work in the reconstruction. Rolf had not really wanted to sell the property to this family but in the end was left no other option. His family could stay on the first floor, where they had always lived; they could use the back courtyard or "Hof" and life could just go on.

Since that time life did just go on, financially things were secure again but the new landlords were much better tenants than owners and much trouble and stress was to follow. Bill asked him who the new owners were and was told Herr and Frau Lange.

X

Life was about to become complicated, extremely complicated. One day several wonderful months into their relationship Christine and Bill were alone together in the living room chatting and playing Mitch Miller records. Juliane was in school, Mutti was in the cellar doing laundry and Rolf was out at his Stammtisch. Somehow their hands came into contact and suddenly they were standing there holding hands, staring each other directly in the eyes. Suddenly Christine became to cry and Bill asked her what was wrong. She answered: "Oh, weh, ich bin verloren!" which means "Woh is me; I'm lost!" She just continued to cry. Bill tried to comfort her and told her for the first time what he had known for a long time that he loved her, totally and hopelessly. She answered that it was the same for her, that she loved him with her whole heart. Then why was she crying? What was wrong?

Just then her mother came into the room and, seeing her daughter crying, ran to her and hugged her and asked her what was wrong. But she too already knew the answer; she too had known it for a long time. She began to cry too. Through her own tears Mutti tried to calm her daughter down and mumbled something about "armer Klaus."

"Who is Klaus, what does he have to do with this?" Savery asked in German. The mother and daughter just continued to cry and hug each other. Suddenly Rolf arrived home and entered the room. He too realized what must have just happened and he simply said: "Oh, weh, das ist alles nicht gut! Ich wusste es!" which meant "Oh, that's not good; I knew it!"

Eventually things quieted down and all four sat down. Christine began to talk in German, still crying. "I didn't mean to fall in love with you. It just happened. You are so different, so wonderful. I couldn't help myself, and now, what do I do?"

"I don't understand," said Bill. "I love you. Is that bad?"

"But what about Klaus?" said Mutti.

"Who is Klaus?"

"Klaus and Christine are engaged. They are supposed to get married in six weeks," said Mutti after a long pause.

"Six weeks! How can that be?" Savery was devastated. How could this be? He had never seen any young man at the Schünemann's. He had never even heard the name Klaus, never heard anyone mention that Christine had a boyfriend. Certainly Christine never mentioned anything. Bill began to cry and he got up, went to Christine and hugged her. "If you love me, just forget him and marry me!"

"That's impossible," said Rolf. "It's already been announced in the paper; she has to marry him."

After some time Mutti told the following story. Klaus was an orphan; his parents had been killed in the war and Klaus was brought up by his aunt and uncle in Esbeck. He met Christine when she was sixteen. Even though he was four years older, a year later they started dating. He had been very protective of her and had kept other boys away from her. She had never gone out with any other boy. After high school Klaus had gone to college and learned banking but he was basically always there in Schöningen. About a year before Bill showed up, the two families had agreed that the two would get married in two years on Christine's twenty second birthday. Christine was not really sure but had agreed to keep her parents happy and he was the only boy she had ever dated.

"Wo IST Klaus?" Savery asked.

"He's in Bavaria in the German border guards, the 'Grenzschutz'," said Mutti. "He hasn't been home in six months but he gets out in eight months and is coming home in six weeks for the wedding."

Savery somehow felt relieved. "Things change; they're not married and they don't have to get married. She loves me! She just told me!"

"Legally they have to get married unless both of them agree to separate because they announced their intentions in the paper. That was before you arrived, Bill," said Mutti in German.

"That makes no sense at all. We'll get that changed, because I love Christine," responded Savery.

The conversation continued for an hour. In the emotional chaos certain things seemed clear. Christine and Bill genuinely loved each other and Klaus would die if he could not marry Christine. It always came back to the fact that the families had agreed and to the fact that Klaus had experienced so much grief as an orphan. It would break his heart. Lucky Klaus. Savery's heart was already broken.

XI

Later that very same night Sergeant Savery was working mids. He was preoccupied with thoughts of Christine and what could be done but otherwise it seemed like a normal night. Sergeant Joe Roetter was just getting off swing shift and the two had a brief conversation.

"Everything normal?" asked Savery.

"Very normal; a slow night so far. We only recorded five conversations in the last two hours. They must be all sleeping over there," said Roetter.

"Mostly Russian or German?"

"Just not much of either," answered Roetter.

"The equipment OK?"

"Everything's OK."

"Any Morse code? You know I'm trying to learn Russian Morse code."

"Yes, I've heard that and no, no Morse code."

"It's a very muggy night; do you think it'll rain?" asked Savery.

"You never know," said Roetter. "See you tomorrow."

The shift began normally. About a half hour in came the high level "Izvestia" Vietnam War transmission. They recorded it and Savery helped his .3 transcribe it and send it on to headquarters. It was a very short article and took little time. By 0230 Archer had

112

recorded three artillery conversations and D'Amico had recorded six conversations, three in German and three in Russian. Three Morse code transmissions were also recorded and processed. All in all a very normal slow night. But it was very hot and Savery took off his fatigue shirt and walked around with his t-shirt on. At around 0245 both D'Amico and Archer asked to be allowed to go home. There were still plenty of linguists present and no work to be done.

After thinking about it, Savery decided to let them go. They left in Archer's VW Beetle. After they left, Savery went to the bathroom. When he came out, he was talking to the soldiers at the receivers, watching them search the frequencies and the gate buzzer went off. Savery picked up the intercom and was told: "Someone's coming up the road; Archer probably forgot something."

Savery walked out to the gate and arrived there just as a jeep was doing the same. The uniformed driver identified himself as a lieutenant from headquarters, Lieutenant Gibson, and showed his I.D. He signed the entry log. Savery identified himself as the shift chief and escorted the lieutenant into the site. He brought him into the main room and introduced him to each soldier and, as he went along, explained what each soldier was doing. While he was there, two conversations were heard and recorded. He showed the lieutenant Corporal Smith typing Russian Morse code and made sure he saw the printed format. Savery even had him turn the radio dial; maybe he could find a transmission. He took him into the transcription room, where Sergeant Fallers was reading a Russian book; there was nothing to transcribe, everything was so slow. They went into the maintenance trailer, where Pfc. Diggins was repairing a receiver. Finally he took the lieutenant outside to see the radar balloon and the clearing and showed him the view of the lights of the nearby East German towns. After the lieutenant went to the bathroom, he said goodbye and left. He had spent one hour and twelve minutes at the site.

Savery told the troops that the lieutenant had left and they were, for some reason, all relieved. They apparently did not like something about him.

The rest of the night got slower and slower and some soldiers actually got into a card game for a half hour just before dawn. Volume did not pick up until around 7 a.m. At 8 a.m. the shift ended and Savery went home and crashed. He did not see Mutti nor Frau Lange. He was exhausted from the day's and the night's events. Yet he did not sleep well but tossed and turned until he got up in the early evening. He showered, put on a fresh uniform and decided to eat at the hotel, where he heard the rumor that Captain Baer was in town. He wondered what was up to have Captain Baer here. He did not go back to Ostendorfstrasse, because he had to sort things out, but, instead, stayed in the hotel until he drove to the site just before midnight.

When he arrived at the site, the gate guard informed him that Captain Baer was here. Sergeant Roetter was standing outside and as he walked by Savery, without actually looking at him, said: "I think Captain Baer is after you."

"Me?" Savery responded.

Entering the main building, Sergeant Savery saw Captain Baer talking in the corner to two lieutenants whom Savery did not know and he went over and saluted. The captain returned the salute and said, "At ease, Sergeant."

"Well, Captain, what brings you here in the middle of the night?"

"Just start your shift; we'll talk then," responded the captain.

Sergeant Savery couldn't imagine why the captain was here but he did as directed. He made sure all soldiers scheduled for night shift had arrived and were at their stations and one by one he let members of the swing shift leave. He talked to the .3's in the transcription room, talked to maintenance, checked with the Morse code operators and finally with the guard at the entry gate. Basically he did what he did at the beginning of every shift. Returning to the captain, he wondered what could possibly be going on.

"So, what's up, Captain?" said Sergeant Savery.

"As you know, Sergeant, Lieutenant Gibson was here last night. Or did you know?"

"Of course, sir. What do you mean? He arrived at around 0300. What about it, sir?"

"After he left, he called me, woke me out of a dead sleep, and told me you were all asleep!"

"What?"

"You heard me. What was going on last night?"

"Nothing was going on and no one was sleeping!"

"We'll see about that. You know this site is a vital component of our early warning defense system. I put you in charge because I felt you were the best for the job. We can't have people sleeping on the job, can we?"

"Of course not, sir. And no one was sleeping."

"Lieutenant Gibson said, he never even saw the person in charge. That means he never saw you."

"What the hell?" blurted out Savery. "I met him at the gate myself."

"That's not what he said. He said he tried to find you, but was escorted around by someone, who tried to lead him away from his inspection of the site."

"I spent the entire time with him myself. Only when he went to the bathroom was he alone."

"That's not what he said at all, Sergeant."

"Where is he? I want to talk to him."

"He's not here but I have two other officers with me and the three of us will get to the heart of the matter."

"There is no heart of the matter; no one was sleeping."

One of the lieutenants came up to the captain and said a few words in his ear, after which the Caption told Savery that they would be using the office in the transcription trailer to conduct interviews and that they would start with him.

If Savery thought the captain was annoying, he thought that the two lieutenants were extremely annoying. They interrogated him for over an hour and wrote down almost everything he said. They constructed a time-line of events which encompassed the entire eight hour shift but which concentrated on the time before and while the lieutenant was at the site. They kept repeating certain points which obviously did not coincide with some things the lieutenant had stated. After they finished, they told Savery to go about his normal routine and not talk to the soldiers about his just completed conversation.

Over the next six hours every member of the shift was called individually into the office and interrogated, some more than once. Captain Baer took part in most of these conversations but for the most part let the two lieutenants conduct the proceedings.

Savery used the time to make sure each soldier was still doing his job and that intelligence gathering was still being done. He also contacted the intelligence sites north and south of Schöningen and discovered that his site had recorded more activity than the other two sites put together. It had been a slow night. All this while they were reportedly sleeping on the job.

Sergeant Savery spoke to Mutti in the hall briefly in the morning before crashing again for the second time in two days. He told her that things were really stressful at the site and that he needed to rest. When he asked about Christine, he was told that she had already left for somewhere to take a picture for the newspaper. Savery told Mutti to please say hello to her from him.

When Sergeant Savery arrived at the site just before midnight, the captain was there again but the lieutenants were gone. He wanted to inform Savery of their conclusions.

"I guess the lieutenant was mistaken for some reason," the captain said. "For some reason he believed that he never saw you and that many of the soldiers were sleeping. I know him personally and I don't believe a lieutenant would lie. That leaves me with a problem and I think I've found a way out."

"What's that, sir?"

"I've decided to give you an Article 15 for not following procedures."

"What do you mean, sir?"

"You allowed Sergeants D'Amico and Archer to go home last night and that's against official protocol. You also allowed Sergeant Fallers to read a Russian novel and that's against protocol."

"But, sir, I've seen that done everywhere, even at headquarters."

"That's the way it will be; you'll get off and the lieutenant did not lie!"

"But the Article 15?"

"You'll be busted to Corporal if you break any more orders in the next three months. In the meantime I'll suspend the punishment. In three months, if you don't break any more orders, the Article 15 will disappear from your record and everything will be back to normal." After a pause, the captain said he was driving back to Kassel and for Savery to have a good night and to just forget what went on, that he still thought Savery was the best man for the job. He ended by saluting and saying "Carry on, Sergeant." He signed out in the entry log at 0038.

During the night basically all shift members were upset and many cursed the lieutenant and even Captain Baer and a week later came word that Archer and D'Amico were being transferred to headquarters. That night some members of the shift sat in the hotel drinking beer and composed a satirical poem about the events of that night.

We hopped into our cars and we rode out to the site,
Swings had just got off, we're gonna work the rest the night,
When up the road this lieutenant comes a riding in his jeep,

117

He comes in the site; he looks around and screams "You're all
    asleep!"
The next day, it was quiet, but the word was, stay on hand,
Then Captain Baer showed up, and the shit, it hit the fan!
They pulled us in the backroom one at a time,
They stood us up, they sat us down, and told us of our crime,
They investigated fully, seems that we were right,
The lieutenant was mistaken; guess this fella's not too bright,
But D'Amico's been zapped to Kassel and Archer's been the same,
And the rest of us they're shipping out, preceded by our fame,
So if you find yourself a working a long and lonely mid,
On any given normal night just as we too did,
And some lieutenant shows up, a looking for someone to screw,
Watch out, 'cause any way you put it, he's gonna screw you.

XII

The next six weeks were hell. Savery did not have his normal enthusiasm for the mission and he just put in his time at the site. He even intentionally "missed" an Izvestia article to voice his displeasure. After all there was no strategic value in them. Frau Lange kept rearranging his personal items in his room. It got to the point, where, every day, Savery would hide some item and she would search his room for that same item when he was away and then leave it on his bed. He spoke to her several times about it but she just grinned and never really directly responded. Maybe she felt it was her right to do so but it really bugged Sergeant Savery and, with things downstairs getting complicated, he started considering moving out. Still he couldn't stand the idea of not seeing Christine every day and he was tortured by thoughts of her upcoming wedding. "How could it be?" he kept asking himself. Mutti and Rolf were as friendly as always but they saw no way out and could offer little help. They did not want to contact Klaus's aunt and uncle. Rolf had a long talk with Bill and told him and he had come to look upon Bill as a son and hoped there was some way for him to marry his daughter but he offered no solution even though Bill kept saying to just tell Klaus goodbye and be done with it. Mutti constantly broke down in tears.

Three weeks before the wedding Klaus came home for two days. He had rented an apartment in town for them to live in and he was there to seal the arrangements. The two soldiers came face to face for the first and only time in the first floor corridor and got into a fierce shouting match and, if not for the Schünemanns, would probably have killed each other on the spot. Christine had confessed to Klaus that she did not love him and that she wanted to get out of the wedding but Klaus would have nothing to do with it. He said that the wedding was long since set and that they were getting married. He said he didn't care about Bill or anyone else. He pleaded with her and with her parents and said they had a binding contract and he would hold them to it.

The day after Klaus left, Savery came home from work to find, that Frau Lange had had a small electric water heater installed under his room sink. She had left a small can on the sink with the word "Wassergeld" written on it. Savery was very annoyed that she had been in his room again. He became very annoyed, when he discovered that she had also searched his room, found a letter to him from America, had obviously tried to read it, and then had not returned it, but left it on his nightstand. He decided he could not take it anymore. He took a paper bag, ripped off a small piece of paper and wrote on it in pencil a message for Frau Lange. He realized that this was probably mean of him but she just didn't seem to get the message that searching through his private things was unacceptable. He folded the note and then slid it under the exposed electrical wires at the door just at eye level, where Frau Lange couldn't miss it exiting the room.

An hour later he heard Frau Lange coming up the stairs and he considered removing the note but did not. Frau Lange rapped on his door and he opened up. She came in, told him about the new water heater and demonstrated it for him. She showed him the money can and told him that electricity was expensive. Therefore he expected Bill to occasionally drop in change to help offset costs. Sergeant Savery told her not to go through his private things but she did not react.

Soon she turned away to exit the room, when she noticed the folded piece of paper under the electrical wire. At first she just stared at it, then started to leave, but immediately stopped, came back in, and took the note out from under the wire. She unfolded it and tried to read it, but didn't have her glasses. She asked Bill to read it to her.

"That is not for you, Frau Lange," Bill said in German.

"Oh, please read it, Bill.'" responded Frau Lange.

"But it's not for you," Savery repeated.

"Oh, please, I don't have my glasses."

"It's not for you, Frau Lange," said Bill a third time.

"Bitte, bitte," repeated Frau Lange, whose curiosity had no bounds.

"OK, if you insist," Savery said one final time in German." It says here: "Du bist eine neugierige Doofe!" which means "You are a nosey stupid person!"

Frau Lange gasped. She grabbed the note and became hysterical and screamed that Bill would have to talk to her husband. She tried to read the note again and then went racing down the hall screaming and yelling for her husband. Soon her husband and she returned to Savery's room and told him, that there would be repercussions for his actions.

Later Mutti asked Bill if anything had happened between him and Frau Lange; for some reason she had been screaming and banging around the house like a crazy person all day long. Savery assured her that nothing had happened.

The following morning Captain Baer called Sergeant Savery at the hotel. He was very upset and kept saying, "What are you doing, self-destructing? "Somehow Frau Lange had personally got through to Captain Baer and now he had to come back to Schöningen to meet with the Langes and Sergeant Savery to straighten out this mess. Another mess! Captain Baer was not happy.

A day later Captain Baer and Sergeant Savery were sitting in Frau Lange's living room, talking about the situation. It was the first time Savery had seen her living room.

Frau Lange was hysterical and acted like a crazy person; Willi just mumbled and mumbled. Frau Lange had several magazines on the table along with Savery's note. She started hysterically talking about her son. Savery suddenly remembered Rolf saying she had a son. He had never heard her son being mentioned since then. It turned out that the Lange's only son had worked for the German federal government in the "guest worker" program. Some five year earlier he had been in Turkey on government business, when he was ambushed by robbers, who stole his car and killed him. Some local Turkish citizens had witnessed the murder and suddenly a group of them had then attacked the robbers and had hanged them on the spot. This had caused a huge sensation in the press and the Lange's had at least 10 newspaper and magazine articles about their son. They had been emotionally crushed by the loss of her son and now this matter with Bill. She just continued to rant and rave hysterically.

Back at the hotel Captain Baer was sympathetic with Sergeant Savery but told him, that he felt Savery should immediately move out. The military had to think about relationships with the local Germans. By coincidence a soldier, who lived in a private room with a private bath in another section of town was leaving in two days and his landlady had asked him to find another tenant if possible. Savery met with the lady and agreed to move in three days hence.

Bill informed the Schünemanns that he was moving out, that he wanted to give them and Christine the privacy they needed at this crucial time. He restated that he truly loved their daughter but that it was out of his hands. There was nothing more he could do; everyone knew where he stood. He promised that he would not come by, would not call them, and that he would not try to contact Christine.

He did have one final conversation with Christine in her living room. He told her again that he loved her and that he was there if anything changed. But for the first time ever he said something mean to her. He asked her if she had ever slept with Klaus. And she answered, a few times but that was all before she knew Bill. Bill responded: "Schläfst du mit jedem?" or "Do you sleep with everyone?' and she answered: "Mit dir bestimmt nicht!" or "Definitely not with you!"

Savery switched rooms ten days before the wedding. His new room was much better than his previous one and the landlady and her husband were super friendly and seemed like really normal people. The room even had a private entrance on the side of the house. The landlady said that no one would ever enter his room when he was not there.

Another hopeless week passed. At work Sergeant Savery tried to get some normalcy back into his life. He was working mids, was still in charge of his shift and was there when two weekly "Izvestia" Vietnam War articles were recorded. He transcribed them and sent them on to headquarters. He heard nothing from anyone at Ostendorfstrasse 24. He somehow imagined that there would be a miracle on the first floor and that there would be relief on the second floor.

Two days before the wedding Sergeant Savery received a call at 0030 hours from Captain Baer on the encoded line.

"What did I do this time?" Savery sarcastically asked.

"Nothing in the last week as far as I know," responded the Captain.

"So, why are you calling?"

"We have a crisis. Up in Gartow there's a confrontation going on at the Elbe!"

"What kind of a crisis?"

"Well, we don't exactly know, that's why we're sending you up, to be our ears."

"What? I can't go now. I have stuff going on."

"You're leaving the site at 0800. The communications truck is already on its way up to you from Kassel."

"But, sir. I really can't go."

"Gehrlach and Cummings will be going with you. They've already been informed."

"But, sir. I really can't go!"

"You're not listening, Sergeant Savery. You ARE going. Sergeant Scott will be taking over your shift. He'll be at the site at 0600 and you can go home and pack some underwear."

"But, sir!" pleaded Sergeant Savery. "I'm not going!"

"You still don't understand. You ARE going and if you don't, I'll have the MPs place you under arrest and I'll demote you! Your Article 15!"

Seeing no way out, Sergeant Savery agreed to go. Sergeant Scott showed up at 0600 and Savery went to his apartment and packed a small bag of toiletries, underwear and one extra fatigue uniform. He noticed his landlady was up and he informed her that he would be gone possibly for a few days.

At 0800 Savery arrived at the site. He had not seen Gehrlach and Cummings for a long time and they were happy to see each other. The communications truck was also there. Gehrlach opened the back door to store their personal gear and, much to everyone's shock, he found three M-1 rifles with many boxes of ammunition. They suddenly realized that maybe there was some real crisis in Gartow.

They decided to take the back roads up to Gartow. They drove through Helmstedt and Grasleben, through Wittingen to Uelzen, before taking their more familiar route the rest of the way to Gartow. During the trip they reminisced about their previous trip to Gartow and Hamburg. They talked about their lives since they last saw each other. Gehrlach and Cummings agreed that their two trips up north were the high point of their German experiences and they wondered if they would see the girls again. Savery said very little about his love life but the other two had heard that he was emotionally involved.

In Uelzen they stopped at a British site and tanked up, had lunch and continued their journey to Gartow. As they got close to Gartow there was much British military traffic on the roads, which the soldiers found unusual. They decided to check in at the Gasthaus before going to the river bank. Captain Baer had managed to get three rooms from Thorsten and Sylvia, who were very happy to see them again. After checking in and asking about Gabi and Liese, the soldiers decided to drive toward Laase, where there was an access to the river bank. All along the road there were British military vehicles. The Americans kept pushing on and finally came to the access point. In a light hearted mood they turned off the road and drove up over the river levy. Crossing the top of the levy and headed down toward the river's edge they were suddenly surprised, shocked and even scared at what they saw. Along each side of the river for as far as one could see, were hundreds of military vehicles facing each other. There were tanks, missile carriers, and every kind of military vehicle.

They were quickly halted by a British military officer, who asked them what to hell they were doing, that this was a critical situation and the last thing they needed was some cowboy playing games. The Americans told the British officer that they had been sent from the 318th to be the US ears on the ground, and that they had been here before so knew their way around. The officer responded that the Americans knew nothing of the situation. This was not a game! Finally the officer calmed down, told the Americans where to park their truck and told them it was OK.

They set up the electronics in their truck and started listening to the East Germans and Russians facing them. Basically all communications were in open German and Russian and it seemed that the other side considered this a real crisis too. Soon they were in communication with Captain Baer, who told them to keep up the good work and to keep him informed of any and all developments. Their rifles were always in the way but the soldiers were careful not to take them out of the truck; there were already hundreds of British, East German, and Soviet soldiers carrying guns.

After talking to the British officer in charge just before dark, they packed up their gear and drove to the "Seehund." The Gasthaus was full of British soldiers and the three soldiers joined some at a large table. At about 10 p.m. who should show up but Gabi and Liese. Bernie and Dave were very surprised and pleased. The girls joined them at the table. They had both just turned seventeen and wanted to celebrate. After about an hour all four of them disappeared.

The next morning at 8 a.m. the soldiers returned to the river bank in a more measured way, where the same officer, seemingly in a better mood, told them where to park and helped them set up. The soldiers were amazed to see so many soldiers and so much military equipment on the Eastern side of the river, just 150 meters away. The reasons for the crisis became clear. The East Germans were dredging out the Elbe River and dumping the dirt on the West German side. The West Germans reacted and starting dredging the river at basically the same spot-dumping the dirt on the East German side. This led to the confrontation and was the crisis. This sounded so unnecessary but it dragged on for another week before both sides just forgot it and retreated from the river bank. As his last act Savery walked down to the river's edge and waved to the border guards on the other side. "What are you doing?" shouted the British officer but the East German guard had already waved back. "I'll be damned!" said the officer.

The three soldiers constantly kept Captain Baer informed and Bernie and Dave lobbied the captain to stay longer but good things have to sometimes end, even here in the 5 kilometer zone. This time all three dreaded going home, Savery to a girl who was probably now married and Gehrlach and Cummings to a future probably without Gabi and Liese.

Captain Baer was at the Schöningen site when they arrived and he thanked them for going a good job, telling Savery that he had restored his faith in him.

XIII

Three weeks went by. Bill had not gone to the Schünemanns at all. He did call them once to say hello and to see how they were but Christine was not mentioned. In fact Bill had no idea where her new apartment was. He assumed that Klaus had returned to Bavaria but he was not even sure about that. Only one thing was certain, that he loved Christine. He spent his spare time by lying around in his private room or walking through the Elm or visiting Waldfrieden, probably hoping to encounter Christine or Mutti, or by visiting the hotel and hanging out with members of his shift. Once he even drove to St. Andreasberg but found no one he had known when he was stationed there. Katia was out of town, visiting an aunt. One afternoon he even went out to the death strip and stared across the border.

One evening just after dark Bill was walking home from the hotel. There was a cold wind and he was hunched over to keep himself warm, when he rounded a corner and bumped squarely into someone rushing the other way. It was Christine. They just stopped and stared at each other for a few moments and suddenly, simultaneously, started to cry and hug each other. For three or four minutes they didn't say a word but showered kisses on each other. Finally they began talking in German.

"I'm sorry I was so mean to you," said Bill. "I didn't mean it."

"I know," she said. "I didn't mean it either."

They stood there and kissed again and again. "What a mess I've made," she said. "What do we do now?"

"Where's Klaus?" asked Bill.

"He's gone back to Bavaria. He was only here for a week."

"Where are you going?"

"Home, I was just at my parents. They're both so sad. I should have listened to you. I don't love him. I love you. My parents know it, Klaus knows it. Everyone knows it. Probably Frau Lange knows it too!" They both chuckled. "Bill, on the day of the wedding, did you ride by the church in a military vehicle?"

"Of course not; I wouldn't do that to you and I was out of town, I was sent up to Gartow for a week."

"When I came out of the church an American army vehicle was going by. I thought it was you and I fainted. It caused quite a scene."

"What do we do now?" asked Bill after a pause.

Christine responded in a strange way, showing her desperation, saying that she was just an insignificant being and that Bill would have to make decisions for her. "Ich bin bloss nur eine winzige arme Armeise. Tu mit mir was du willst!"

After standing for ten minutes at the street corner, Bill decided to walk her home and she directed him in the correct direction but when they got to her street, they hesitated and did not want to separate. Christine said that she did not want to leave him and suggested that he show her where he lived. And so they changed directions and walked the five blocks to his new residence. They stood outside in the darkness, hugged and kissed and Bill finally told her that he wanted her to spend the night with him. She simply responded: "Ich bin bereit; ich liebe dich." which meant "I'm ready; I love you!"

They entered his room through the private entrance. His landlady had left two candles on his night stand and they lit them. Soon they were sitting on his bed gently caressing each other in the candle light.

For them all sense of right and wrong disappeared. They were the only people on earth; their love was the only truth that existed. It wasn't about sex; it was about love, their love for each other. After a few moments, looking straight in each other's eyes and not speaking a word, they both stripped and got into bed. They lay there for an hour, just holding, caressing, crying, smiling, reliving. Finally they made love and for the first time in his life, Bill was totally happy. He hoped that this happiness would never go away.

Hours went by and, awakening, they realized that morning had arrived all too soon. What would they do; what should they do?

Christine told Bill how much she loved him and suddenly told him that she was pregnant, saying "Ich bin mit Kind."

Bill was shocked and, even though he hated saying the name, responded: "With Klaus's child? Why didn't you tell me before?"

"No, not with his child, with your child!"

"That makes no sense, how can that be?"

"I feel it," she said. "I'm having your baby!"

"But how can you feel that?"

"I just feel it and I want to have your baby. I'm so happy. I love you so much!"

At about 10 a.m. they separated for the day, after agreeing to meet again at 8 p.m. at Bill's apartment.

XIV

B ill had to go to a meeting at the site and Christine had to go to work at the newspaper office until 5 p.m. She was getting promoted and would conduct interviews for major stories. She said with a laugh that she loved her job almost as much as she loved Bill. She told Bill to drop in and see her parents, that they missed him very much.

After the meeting Bill did call Mutti and tell her that he wanted to drop by. She consulted with Rolf, who had just returned from his Stammtisch, and he too thought it was OK. Bill went over, after eating at the hotel. It was good to see them and Rolf said, that he wished things had worked out differently than they did.

Mutti and Bill played a couple games of chess, which Bill once again won but it brought laughter back into the house. While he was there, their next door neighbor, Herr Kraft, came by with some homemade pastry. He watched them play chess for a moment. Mutti told him that Bill and she had played hundreds of matches and that Bill had won every single match. Herr Kraft, who was the chess champion of Schöningen, said he would like to play Bill to see how good he really was. They started the game and within a few moves, Herr Kraft had taken most of Bill's pieces away and after a move said "Checkmate!" Herr Kraft was suddenly embarrassed that he had beaten Bill so decisively and easily and he suggested that they switch sides and continue the game. Bill said that that would be unfair, because Herr Kraft would have only a couple pieces and two pawns to play with. Herr Kraft insisted and the game continued. Somehow Savery captured Kraft's rook and the game was over. Savery had somehow won. Herr Kraft was not amused but was gracious and said that they would have to play sometime again in the future.

At 8 p.m. they were together again in Bill's apartment. They hugged and kissed each other and soon they were in bed together again but in this night they did not cry. They both seemed to have come to the conclusion and they would work it out and would somehow be together for the rest of their lives. Love would find a way. Christine was convinced that she was strong enough; she had got them into this mess, and she would get them out of it, Bill pressed his ear into her stomach to listen to the baby and she responded by saying: "Don't be crazy, the baby's too small to move, but it's there and I know it's your child." It was a very emotional romantic night.

In fact many, many romantic nights would follow and the happiness did not go away. The two lovers managed to see each other every single day. The Schünemanns noticed that Christine had changed and was suddenly very happy. They had no idea that she and Bill had been together. One day Mutti too encountered Bill on the street and point blank asked him if he had seen her daughter but Bill avoided a direct answer.

One afternoon there was a big party at the hotel. Sergeant Baker was getting discharged and was leaving within a week. He was going to the US military hospital complex in Giessen down near Frankfurt for his discharge physical, then coming back for a couple weeks before leaving for the States. Captain Baer was attempting to convince him to reenlist for another three years. He was already an E-5 and would probably be guaranteed E-6. With the Vietnam War building momentum, recruits were becoming hard to find and the military needed well trained soldiers here in Germany. Although nothing was written in stone, Baker would probably just continue on in his intelligence gathering duties in Germany. He had become after all one of the best Russian .3's in the military in Germany. The military had just instituted a bonus program to get soldiers to reenlist and Baker would get more than four thousand dollars cash.

Savery recalled those NATO maneuvers more than a year ago, where Baker, D'Amico and Savery had played with the radios after being tear gassed and he wondered if Captain Baer would be trying to convince Baker to reenlist if he knew. He also thought of D'Amico and what he was doing after being transferred to Kassel.

While reliving some of their exploits, including their fun in St. Andreasberg, Savery suddenly realized for the first time that his enlistment was also almost up. He had just over three months to go. This realization sobered him up and he became very quiet. He didn't want his enlistment to end; he didn't want to go home or to Vietnam or anywhere, he wanted to stay here, he wanted everything to remain exactly as it was. He wanted to stay totally happy. Why did things always have to change?

The following week Sergeant Savery was working the swing shift. As always there was very little East German or Russian radio activity. Throughout the shift the .1's at the receivers had recorded more than two dozen transmissions but they were all very short radio checks and had absolutely nothing of intelligence importance. Never the less the .3's had transcribed them all word for word and had sent them on to headquarters.

By about 2300 the soldiers were thinking about getting off work. They started talking about going to the hotel and drinking. They hoped that some girls would be there to guarantee their happiness. Even Sergeant Savery was thinking about Christine; in fact, he had been thinking about her for hours, hoping and expecting to be soon lying in her arms. One of the .1's was searching the dials way up at the high end where there was never any activity. He was bored and was just going through the motions. He picked up some voice traffic and started recording it. After about ten minutes Savery went over to him and asked him what he was recording, some artillery unit? The sergeant responded that he wasn't sure, that he wasn't even sure if it was Russian, that he was just recording it for something to do. Savery told him to have fun. This was not all that unusual. The site often picked up taxi traffic from East Berlin or even once from Moscow through some fluke in the atmosphere. But after two more minutes Sergeant Savery decided to listen in.

At first the transmission was very garbled but Savery thought he heard the Russian word for plane "samolyot." Immediately he heard another voice saying: "On gorit; on padaet!" or "It's burning; it's falling!"

Savery couldn't believe his ears; had he just heard a plane shot down? His mind raced and he knew from his training back in Virginia that he was correct: the Soviets had shot down a plane. Savery told the sergeant to keep recording no matter what, and ran into the communications trailer. Corporal Ligotti was sitting there, leaning back with his feet up on this desk, reading a German newspaper.

"Send a critic!" Savery yelled.

"Yeah, right," responded Ligotti.

"Send it, damn it!" Savery screamed and kicked Corporal Ligotti.

Ligotti had never sent a critic; as far as he knew the site had never sent a critic. A critic wasn't anything to play with. A critic was the highest form of emergency message, designed to reach the President of the United States anywhere in the world he happened to be within four minutes. Ligotti had repeatedly practiced sending them but never expected to actually send one.

He turned on the machine and fed in the tickertape. The teletype started clicking and suddenly there was a pause. "What's the message?" he asked.

"Plane shot down!" responded Savery. Ligotti hesitated. "DO it!' yelled Savery.

Ligotti typed it in and sent the message. Within one minute came a response from Intelligence Headquarters Europe: "Who says?"

"Send just 'Savery'!" Savery told Ligotti.

Savery went back to the receiver; the garbled conversation was still going on, and he told the sergeant to keep recording. He directed another station to also start recording the same conversation.

Within ten minutes Captain Baer was on the phone. He patched Savery over to Burt Nelson, who was still in the Ice House in Kassel. After a brief conversation they were both in agreement that a plane, some plane, somewhere, had been just shot down by the Soviets. One odd aspect of the event was that no one else, not one single intelligence gathering station along the border, not the US, not the British, was hearing or reporting the incident.

Soon all communications channels with Kassel and with Intelligence Headquarters were open with more and more persons asking for information but Savery could not add much. He was just sure of what he had reported. Captain Baer told Savery to stay on duty and supervise the site's activities and that the wheels were already turning, thanks to the site's critic. He also said that he and Burt Nelson were on their way and would be there within two and a half hours.

The mids shift arrived and the swings shift was allowed to leave, all except the two sergeants manning the receivers recording the Russian conversations. But most did not want to leave and, in fact, the entire shift stayed to see what Captain Baer and Burt Nelson would say.

By the time they arrived, the news had reached the correct people and the entire intelligence community was involved, searching for a downed plane. Burt Nelson listened to the entire garbled Russian tape and apparently understood most all of it. He identified one voice as being the pilot of a Soviet fighter and two other voices were familiar to him but he wasn't sure from where. He was sure that one voice had said in Russian: "That will show them!"

Captain Baer and Burt Nelson were only at the site for an hour and left to return back to headquarters with the tapes. Captain Baer was very friendly, thanking the shift for its good work. He told Sergeant Savery to go home and get some rest.

Two weeks later Captain Baer sent a message that there would be a follow up meeting for all seventy nine troops the next day at noon at the site. At the meeting he told the troops that, because of the site's critic message, lives had been saved. A US recognizance plane way up north over the Sea of Murmansk was patrolling the Soviet border, where it intentionally entered Soviet air space. The goal was to force the Soviets to turn on their emergency radar system. Once they did this, the US plane would chart their locations and then turn around and get out into international air space. But this time the Russians scrambled their jets and, upon orders directly from the Politburo of the Soviet Union, they had shot down the American plane. Burt Nelson had positively identified the voices of two Politburo members. Once the US air base in Norway realized through the critic that a plane and been shot down and realizing that they had not heard from their plane at the scheduled time, rescue seaplanes were sent out. As a result, all five airmen, floating in a raft in international waters, were rescued.

Savery, hearing this, thought one thing: border games!

Captain Baer ended his presentation with a sincere thanks to the site, saying he had one further announcement. He called Sergeant Savery to the front, presented him with an envelope and told him to open it. Inside were chevrons of an E-6. Sergeant Savery had been promoted to Specialist 6. The meeting erupted in applause.

Captain Baer shook hands with SPC-6 Savery and told him that he was always sure Savery was the right man for the job. He concluded his conversation by saying that he had personally expunged the Article 15 from Savery's record and that he still expected bigger things from the staff sergeant. For the first time he even mentioned reenlistment options for Savery, saying that he could guarantee him that he would stay right here at the 318th and that, because of his E-6 rank, his bonus would be over six thousand dollars. Savery was hesitant to discuss this and the captain sensed it and said that they would talk later.

In fact, E-6 Savery was very proud of what he had done. Unlike breaking the Warsaw Pact code fifteen months earlier, which had been pure luck and coincidence, this time it was his knowledge and experience and he deserved his promotion.

For some reason he started thinking about his old friend Richard Williams, Willi the Bag, E-6 Williams and wondered exactly what he must have done to be promoted so high. He theorized that Rich must have done something truly important and significant. Savery had known a few E-6's but none except for Rich and himself on their first enlistments.

During his last weeks in the military SPC-6 Savery had to make many decisions: was he going to reenlist, was he going back to America, what of Christine? Captain Baer contacted him almost every day, trying to convince him to stay in the military. The army needed soldiers like him, he was repeatedly told. He would stay right here on the job and nothing would change. But Savery was not convinced. Baker had reenlisted and after weeks of uncertainty had been shipped to Vietnam after all. Savery did not want that and that alone caused him to refuse to reenlist. Captain Baer came up with a compromise. He suggested that Savery separate from active duty and stay in Germany for a few months, think things over and then within six month reenlist. He would receive separation pay, enough to support him for a few months and then if he reupped, he would get more than a six thousand dollar bonus and, if he did not, he would get free transportation home.

Bill discussed the options with Christine and decided to remain as a civilian in Germany. Two weeks before his enlistment ended, he went by military train to Giessen to take his separation physical.

His hearing test went exactly the way his initial hearing test had gone. The technician giving the hearing test was very impressed by his hearing and, in fact, had heard of Savery's connection with the spy plane incident. The technician even referred to him as "golden Ears." Savery wondered if that was a standard phrase. From Giessen SPC-6 Savery went to the US Consulate in Frankfurt and obtained a passport. After a week he was back in Schöningen, where he applied for German plates for his car. He also had a long talk with his landlady about keeping his room for a number of months and she was very understanding and agreeable. Finally Savery had a big party at the hotel. Everyone and anyone was invited and Savery got drunk. Of course Christine did not attend.

Life out of the military was immediately different. Savery could not go to the site anymore and no one would even discuss what went on there. One night a whole series of flares went up just over the border in East Germany and Savery imagined another escape attempt but, try as he would, Savery could not get anyone to say even one word about it. Savery found himself repeatedly visiting the death strip just to keep in touch with his reality. Not that the soldiers were unfriendly. Just the opposite, his friends were friendlier than ever and he hung out more and more with them. Christine was often working and started staying overnight in her own apartment when Bill was out of town. And Bill was out of town a lot. Because he was bored and in many ways isolated but also curious, he started taking car trips away from Schöningen for a few days at a time. Three different times he drove to Amsterdam just to have a delicious Polynesian meal called Rice Table. It consisted of white rice and up to 23 side dishes of herbs and spices. It was worth the five hour drive.

Once he even drove all the way to Copenhagen just to see it and its famed amusement park "Tivoli Gardens," that Rich Williams had raved about. He was correct; all the girls had white blond hair. Savery also saw the mermaid statue in the harbor and farther north

McBeth's castle, Helsingor. Savery even wandered around in the castle and pretended to be McBeth. Coming south from Copenhagen, Savery entered Germany via ferry boat at Puttgarden, Germany. To his surprise he was detained for hours. The border police were convinced that Savery was carrying concealed drugs somewhere in his VW. They stripped basically everything from the car, including the battery, engine parts, seats, door panels, wheels, even the gas tank was taken out of the car. After two hours all they found was a new, sealed glass jar of Maxwell House coffee. One policeman held the jar, inspecting it, turning it, shaking it for at least one hour. Finally they reluctantly replaced the gas tank and put the wheels back on the car and lent Savery wrenches to rebuild the rest, but were still convinced they had missed a big drug shipment. Finally leaving the entry point Savery was going to visit the East/West German border at Lubeck but lost his enthusiasm and just drove back to Schöningen.

Savery spent more and more time traveling. He went as far west as Flanders Field in Belgium to see the crosses row on row and as far south as Barcelona, Spain and Venice, Italy. It was in Venice, two weeks into this excursion, that Savery suddenly realized that he shouldn't be there but in Schöningen. It seemed to him that every highway was leading him farther away. He drove from Venice fourteen hours to get back home to be with Christine, who jokingly said, that she was starting to wonder if he would ever return.

Christine was looking more and more pregnant and Bill couldn't help still wondering if it were his child. She was joyfully insistent: "Don't be silly; of course it's your child, our child!"

It had somehow already become summer and Bill wanted to take one more trip, a trip to Berlin. He wanted to see East Berlin to see what life was like behind the Wall. His landlady had told him that her family had an apartment in West Berlin and that Bill could stay there for a couple days. In the middle of June 1967 Bill drove to Berlin along the same middle corridor that he had traveled as a soldier. The trip was uneventful and he found the apartment in a side street in Berlin just across from Charlottenburg Palace. The first morning there Bill went to Friederichstrasse and crossed into East Berlin. Two things really seemed noticeable to him. The first was the smell of two cycle engines and the second was the presence of thousands of Soviet troops in uniform. It seemed that the East German policemen were reasonably friendly but that the Soviets seemed confrontational. Savery was very careful to avoid being noticed. He looked at Checkpoint Charlie from the East but it was difficult to get very close. He had lunch in a restaurant near the Pergamum Museum. The waiter seamed friendly but Savery had to wait for a half hour for service. During this time Savery just watched a table of about ten Soviet officers. Finally after they left, the waiter came over to Bill in a very friendly way and apologized for the delay. He was waiting for the soldiers to leave. The waiter suddenly started to speak English. "I want your sunglasses. How much will you take for them?"

"They're not for sale," said Savery.

"We don't have sunglasses here. I really will give you anything for them. A free meal? 100 Marks?"

"They're not for sale," repeated Savery. "But, I'll tell you what. You can just have them. They're my present to you!"

"Oh thank you, thank you," repeated the waiter and put the sunglasses on his face. "Now I look like Elvis Presley!"

After a brief visit to the museum Savery returned by underground at Friederichstrasse to his apartment in West Berlin. He decided that night to spend one more day in Berlin before returning to West Germany and Schöningen. He ate dinner in a small Turkish restaurant near the apartment. His plan for the next day was to see the Charlottenburg palace grounds and then go downtown to the new opera house and then to Checkpoint Charlie for one last look. At 10 a.m. he left the apartment and walked down the side street toward the palace grounds. When he got to the main boulevard in front of the palace, he saw something he had never seen before. Along the side of the street in both directions as far as one could see were endless police trucks, each carrying ten riot policemen. Savery was shocked and almost afraid but they just ignored him and he tried to ignore them. Crossing the boulevard, Savery became aware that hundreds of civilians were staring at the police trucks, wondering what was going on. Savery entered the palace grounds and wandered around for about an hour. When he came out, the police trucks and policemen were gone. He entered a bus going in the general direction of the opera house and just before his destination the streets were blocked by police and all passengers were ordered to get off.

One could hear chanting and shouting not far away and there were police and young people everywhere. Suddenly shots rang out around the corner and protesters and police started chasing each other and throwing missiles at each other. Savery was not interested in getting any closer but instead retreated down a side street away from the action and eventually boarded a bus headed in the opposite direction. It turned out that the protesters were demonstrating against the Vietnam War and against the visit to Berlin of the Shah of Iran. Several police and protesters were injured and one protester had been shot and killed by police. His name was Benno Ohnesorg and was from Hannover. Savery, who was glad to be away from the action, eventually found his way to Checkpoint Charlie and via a roundabout way back to his apartment. The next morning he left Berlin and returned to Schöningen.

Several days later Christine and he were taking a ride away from Schöningen so that they could be together in public. They ended up in Braunschweig at an art miuseum. Above a stairway landing between the first and second floor was a huge pastoral painting from the eighteenth century. They stopped, stared at the picture and joked about the many cows, when suddenly they noticed that the painter was someone named Savery. They laughed and laughed about the artist and said that they had found Bill's ancestors. Later they drove to Hannover, where they visited a small lake and rented a rowboat. About a half hour later a funeral procession with hundreds of walking mourners went through the park following a black hearse. It was the funeral procession for Benno Ohnesorg. It became clearer and clearer that their relationship could not exist in a vacuum; that reality, society's reality, would not permit them to just carry on. This led to a long tearful discussion between the two about their future together.

Christine told Bill that she had to work things out on her own, that her husband was returning soon, and that Bill had to leave Germany and her so that she could figure things out and make the right decisions; she had already made things such a mess. Bill responded that he had helped create the mess but he would do whatever she wanted him to do. After a very long discussion, Bill promised to contact the military the following day and get a flight back to America. It turned out to be a very sad day.

The following morning Savery called military headquarters in Frankfurt and after a few conversations was informed that he would leave Frankfurt, Germany four days hence. So soon!

During the next days he checked out of his Privatzimmer, sold his car, said goodbye to a few friends, visited the Schünemanns and finally Christine and then, having received orders through the site in Schöningen, left Germany via a commercial TWA flight. If he had realized what the future would hold, he might not have gone. His thoughts on the flight were about his entire time in Germany from the sweet smell of Chestnut blossoms, to the many towns along the border zone, to his relationship with Christine. He had truly come to love the people he had met and that love would last a life time.

Epilog

ivilian Bill Savery arrived in his hometown at the end of August 1967 exactly one week after the beginning of the fall semester at the University of Vermont.

He had already stopped in New York City for three days, where he had visited the United Nations and had tried to apply for a job as a Russian interpreter. He was directed to the US delegation. Every one there was very friendly and he managed to get three interviews. At each interview he had to speak Russian, translate Russian articles from Isvestia and give a simultaneous translation of videotaped speeches by the Russian ambassador. Savery thought he had done an excellent job and fully expected to be offered a position on the spot but of course he was not. When he asked how come, one delegation member told him that, although Savery was good, he knew dozens of applicants just as good. It was suggested that he first get a college degree and then reapply at the UN or apply to the CIA or FBI. They were always looking for people with Savery's background.

On his first day home, a Friday, Savery borrowed a car and drove the 80 miles to the university to apply for entrance. He was turned down because the semester had already started but after several interviews and meetings on that very day he was admitted. The underlying reason was that he was just coming from military service.

He would be in Liberal Arts and was told to contact a Dr. James White, chairman of the Foreign Language Department.

He found Dr. White in his office and the two talked for a few minutes. The professor said that the best way to determine Savery's ability and therefore correct placement in German and Russian was to take a test in each. The exam was a standardized 120 question multiple choice test. Sixty questions were reading comprehension and sixty were taped listening comprehension. This test was called the Yale Test for Foreign Language Ability and was traditionally given at the end of the second full year of language study. Dr. White suggested that Savery take each test on that very day and that he would stay and supervise the process. Savery agreed. Dr. White cleared a table in his office and the test in German was given, followed by the test in Russian. Two and a half hours later the tests were over and Dr. White said that he would check the results the following day, but then, perhaps out of curiosity or just because Savery was there, decided to check the results with him still in the office. He went to a locked file and brought back an answer key and placed it over the just completed Russian exam. To Dr. White's utter surprise, Savery had answered all 120 questions correctly. Dr. White said that he had never had anyone even come close to that result and if he hadn't been in the room, he would have thought that Savery had somehow cheated. He decided to check the results of the German test. He placed the German master template over the just completed test. He exclaimed: "My God, I think they're all right too!" He looked more closely and said: "No, you missed one!"

"Number sixty-seven?" Savery asked.

"Yes, how did you know?" asked Dr. White.

"Because that's the only one I guessed at; I knew the rest."

Thus began the academic phase of Savery's young life. Due to 38 transfer credits in Russian and thanks to taking seven or even eight courses per semester he managed to graduate with a Bachelor's degree in German and Russian in two years instead of four.

Dr. White had aided Savery in becoming an unpaid teaching assistant in German and Russian and finally helped him get accepted into Graduate School at the State University of New York in Buffalo. And so it was that Savery and five other graduate students and a professor of German, Dr. David Richards, were sent to the University at Cologne, Germany for the 1971-1972 academic year, four long years after leaving Christine behind. Years in which Bill made many important, life altering decisions and every choice he made was in many ways wrong and brought him farther away from any real happiness. And worst of all, he knew each choice was wrong when he made it but he did it anyway. But during these four long years he had never stopped thinking about what he had lost and he wondered if Christine ever thought of him, was she happy or was she as miserable as he was, did she have more kids, was she still married, had she gone on in her career, had she moved and what of her parents? Were they even still alive? What he knew for sure was that he wanted to, had to, see her again. He should have returned years before, or not have left at all. So many bad decisions!

In all these years there had been only one letter from Christine and that had been way back in the beginning. In the letter she had said that the baby was due any day, that she could handle any problem, and that she was looking forward to being together and would write again soon.

Within a week of arriving in Cologne, the students were matriculated at the university and living in student dormitories in Hahnenstrasse.

Dr. Richards had arranged for the group to take a four day train trip to West Berlin. Savery found the border crossing at Helmstedt to be totally unchanged and in fact found Berlin to be also unchanged except he found the mood in West Berlin to be much more positive.

The Wall at Checkpoint Charlie was totally painted with political graffiti. He heard West Berlin positively referred to as "die Inselstadt" or Island City. Willi Brandt, who had been the mayor of West Berlin four years earlier, was now the Federal Chancellor of Germany. For the second time Savery crossed underground through the "Geisterbahnhof" at Checkpoint Charlie into East Berlin, where he realized how dire the situation was there. He longed to see the five kilometer zone to see how it had changed.

Leaving Berlin on the return trip he decided to exit the train in Helmstedt, rent a car to see his favorite border spots and visit the Schünemanns. Dr. Richards was OK with this and Savery called the Schünemanns and told Mutti he would be arriving the following day.

In Helmstedt he rented a VW Beetle and drove to Checkpoint Alpha. It was totally the same; even the restaurant at the plaza had the same waitresses. Savery walked from the plaza through the woods along the death strip in the direction of the bomb factory. The path was still there but the bomb factory was abandoned; the soldiers long gone. Savery returned to his rented vehicle and drove to Bahrdorf and the "Spargel." The site was gone; the barbed wire was gone; the whole place looked like a ruin. But the "Spargel" was doing well and Horst and Gabi, now with a small child, remembered Savery fondly. Nina had long since got married and had resettled in Wolfsburg. Savery was happy to hear that she had got her life together. At several points along the death strip Savery waved at the East German guards on the other side but not one single guard ever waved back. Finally Savery made his way to Schöningen and got a room overnight at the hotel, which was still brimming with soldiers. The Gasthaus was still full of young girls and life seemed to be exactly the same. No one was there from before but several troops knew the name Savery and the incident of the shot down plane. It was still the only critic the site had ever sent. Captain Baer had long since been sent to Vietnam.

Savery walked past his old apartment and then Ostendorfstrasse 24 but the Schünemanns did not live there any longer. Surprised by this news, Savery called them and was told their new address on the edge of town in state subsidized housing. Savery said that he would be there at 11 a.m. the following day. Savery had a beer and went to bed.

The next morning, carrying flowers, Savery arrived at Schünemann's apartment. Mutti and Rolf opened the door and soon all three were crying and laughing and remembering. There were a million questions and explanations. Rolf was proud of his growing stamp collection and showed Bill his entire collection which now numbered in the tens of thousands of stamps. He even gave Bill about 50 stamps and told him to guard these stamps, that someday they would be worth a fortune. Rolf no longer went to his "Stammtisch" because he couldn't walk that far and he seldom had money for a taxi, which Mutti contradicted, saying he just wanted to stay with her.

Eventually the three went to the cherry wine restaurant Waldfrieden for lunch and a glass of Kirschwein. When they got in the car, Rolf warned Bill of a new road sign. Instead of a big rectangle with the word HALT, there was now a hex angle with the international word STOP. Bill thanked him for the information. At lunch the discussion continued endlessly. Juliane now lived in Würzburg and owned an American made jeep. She had a German boyfriend and they were thinking of getting married. Herr Lange, Willi, had died shortly after Bill had left, a year later Frau Lange, too. The house was sold and the new owners wanted the Schünemanns to move out along with a couple American soldiers who lived there, so the Schünemanns had moved into subsidized housing and were very content and free from constant bother.

For the entire four hours together one topic never came up: Christine. Bill couldn't take it any longer. Although he loved the parents, his real reason for being there was the daughter. Over a third glass of Kirschwein Bill finally asked about her. At first they didn't want to talk about her but slowly through prodding they spoke more and more about their daughter. She had landed a position as a radio/TV reporter in Hannover and after commuting by train for a year from Schöningen, while Klaus was still in the border guards, they had bought an apartment in Hannover, where they still lived. Christine had given birth to a beautiful girl. Six months after the birth she informed Klaus that she was leaving him. Klaus had prevented that by getting a lawyer to gain custody of the child if she did leave. A few months later Christine had tried to overdose and commit suicide but she was discovered, brought to the hospital and she survived. Savery thought back to his growing academic achievements during this time, while the truly important events were going on totally unbeknownst to him. He wondered why he had not tried to contact her and he could only blame himself. Through a painful recovery, she managed to keep her job and had in fact advanced in her profession but had been forced to stay with Klaus, who had become vice-president of a bank in Hannover. It was that or lose her child too. So they had remained together in an unhappy union for these past four years.

In fact they had had a second baby, a boy, a year ago. He was in very poor health because he had a heart defect. During this long discussion Mutti and Rolf wondered out loud if the baby might have been Bill's and asked him directly if he and Christine had ever slept together. For Christine's sake Bill avoided a direct answer but could only imagine the difficult position Christine was in totally alone. In the conversation Rolf repeatedly told Bill that he wished Bill had married his daughter, that he was sure everything would have been better. Before Bill left for the long drive back to Cologne, Mutti gave him Christine's telephone number and address in Hannover. She told him that he should see Christine so that they could work things out face to face. She wanted her daughter to find some kind of happiness.

A week later, well rested but very nervous, Bill entered a phone booth in a Cologne post office and called Christine's number. He had practiced every possible conversation and knew he had to talk with her, to see her, and straighten everything out. She answered the phone and it was obvious that she knew Bill was in Germany. Mutti had spoken with her about Bill's visit. At first the German conversation went well.

"Oh, there you are. Where have you been?"

"I've missed you. I'm sorry for all the pain I've caused you."

"Pain, yes, I've had a lot of pain."

"I've just been in Schöningen."

"I know; I just talked to my mother."

"Ich will dich sehen," Bill said in German meaning "I want to see you" but used a strong word for want, which normally indicated that one was sure to get what one wanted.

"Du WILLST, du WILLST mich sehen!" she said with an angry annoyed voice. "Das WIRST du aber nicht. Nie!" meaning "But you will not. Never!"

She hung up. Bill was devastated; he repeated to himself over and over what he had said to make her so upset. He still didn't understand the power of his words. Minutes later he realized that he should have used the more polite expression: "ich möchte dich sehen," meaning: "I would like to see you." But the damage had been done; it was too late.

More than a semester went by and spring had sprung. Bill had talked to Mutti by phone several times but she did not want to talk about Christine. In their last conversation she did say that her daughter was having a tough time. Bill decided to call Christine again. This time the result was better.

"I'm sorry I upset you before," Bill said. "I didn't want to; that's the last thing I wanted."

"I'm sorry too," she answered. "I wish I had not hung up. We've wasted so much time."

"I should have called you right back but I didn't dare."

"I really wanted to see you when you called me last fall. I couldn't call you back because I didn't know your address or your telephone number. I still don't."

"Please don't take this the wrong way but I really want to see you. We have so much to talk about and it should be face to face."

"Do you know that I have a son? Poor Klausi has a heart condition and needs an operation."

"Yes, your mother told me. I would like to see you anyway. We have to; we've gone through so much together."

"OK, we'll try it, but under the following condition. Every Wednesday I take the kids to the Freizeitheim in Herrenhausen. Our daughter plays with her friends there and Klausi just crawls around. Could you be there by noon? You know where it is; we went boating there once."

"That is perfect. It's only three hours and I'll leave early so I'll be there on time. At noon Bill was outside the Freizeitheim. He went in the building but could not find them. He went outside to a climbing area for kids but he still couldn't find them. Finally after searching around for ten minutes, he just sat down and wondered what to do next. He started thinking that she had changed her mind, when a black haired lady pushing a baby carriage and leading a four-year-old girl entered the climbing area. She hesitated, looked around, then came in his direction. He looked at them and then continued his search for Christine. The lady walked right up to him. It was Christine. Shocked, Bill stood up.

"You've changed," he said.

"You have, too," she responded. "I almost didn't recognize you." Bill suddenly realized that he had indeed changed greatly from four years earlier, when he was just starting to let his hair and his beard grow after getting out of the Army. And now his hair was over his shoulders and he had a full although straggly beard.

Her little daughter suddenly said to Bill: "Du bist ein Seeräuber," meaning "You are a pirate!"

Bill answered: "Und du bist aber schön, Mädchen!" meaning "And you are very pretty, girl!"

"Seeräuber, Seeräuber," she giggled. Bill found the child indeed very pretty and he searched her face for any resemblance to his own but only found her mother's face. Christine told her to go play with her friends and then picked up her son into her arms and presented him to Bill.

"You really do look so different, I remember you so different."

"Maybe it's my wig," she said. "I didn't know what to expect, I didn't know how to dress so I decided to wear this old wig."

"Could you please take it off?"

"My hair's a mess," she warned him. Bill took a chance and gently placed his hands on her wig and pulled it off. Her long light brown hair tumbled down and glistened in the sunshine and the features of her beautiful face filled Bill's senses. She was still the strikingly beautiful girl he remembered, maybe even more beautiful.

They talked for about two hours, being very careful that the children didn't notice anything unusual. As they talked they became more and more comfortable with each other and it was clear to each that they were still in love after all these years. Finally they had to separate because she had to go to work at the TV station for the evening news broadcast. They agreed to meet the following Monday at 11 a.m. at the same place in Hannover.

Bill waited in Hannover for four hours after they separated just for the chance to see her on the evening news. She was beautiful on screen but more so she was good. She looked like a movie star and sounded like a professional reporter. Her story was about Willi Brandt and his new policy regarding East and West Germany called "Ostpolitik." Christine had truly come a long way in her career.

At 10:45 the next Monday Bill was at the Freizeitheim; once again he had skipped a couple courses but for once he realized that some things were more important than academics. Christine arrived five minutes later dressed as herself, a beautiful young movie star woman.

"Where are your kids?" asked Bill.

"My sister Juliane has taken them to Grandma and Grandpa's for the day. We're all alone."

The two drank a cup of coffee from the cafeteria and sat and talked. "Where's Klaus?"

"He's where he always is, at work. Twelve hours a day. That's all he cares about. I take care of the children; he works. When I'm at work, I have a babysitter with the children."

After the coffee Christine invited Bill to see their apartment and Bill asked if that was a good idea. She just answered that Bill should just trust her. Their apartment was spacious and was decorated with pictures from Christine's reporting. There was even a picture of her with Willi Brandt. They talked very honestly for hours. Christine explained that Klaus knew their daughter was not his; that he didn't care. Their second child just happened. She said that she had done what she always did when having sex with her husband; pretend she was sleeping with Bill. Bill said that, because she was so beautiful, many men must have desired her and she answered that, indeed, while doing her job as a reporter, many men, many good looking, important men had made moves on her but that she had always refused, not because of Klaus, but because she was remaining true to Bill. It was clear that she could never leave her kids and clear that Bill could never permanently move to Germany. But they promised to remember forever their love for each other. They said goodbye with a long loving hug and many tears and they parted, expecting to never see each other again.

Two weeks later there was a vote of confidence for Willi Brandt and his new "Ostpolitik" in the German parliament. The TV room at the student dorms on Hahnenstrasse in Cologne was crammed full with hundreds of students all supporting Brandt and hoping to see normalization of tensions between the two countries. Bill was there too but he was hoping to see Christine on TV. Brandt's opponent was named Rainer Barzel and he wanted to topple Brandt's coalition government and become chancellor himself. The vote was very close and came down to one delegate, who was in the hospital and was being transported by ambulance to parliament to vote against Brandt. As it turned out, by pure coincidence, reiner Zufall, there had been a car accident and the delegate did not get to the parliament on time and so by one vote Willi Brandt stayed in power. As the reporter was saying this on TV, Savery yelled out: "Lieber reiner Zufall, als Rainer Barzel!" meaning "Preferably pure coincidence than Rainer Barzel!" Students immediately erupted in applause, students came up to Savery and shook hands with him and patted him on the back. In fact, over the next few weeks many students at the university asked if he had been the foreign student who had uttered those lines.

So in the Spring of 1972 relations between East and West Germany finally normalized, which meant, among other things, that West Germany officially recognized East Germany as an independent country. Savery wondered what this would mean for the five kilometer zone and its people whom he had grown to love so. He was certain that it would eventually mean big change and he knew all too well that not all change was good.

A week later Dr. Richards announced that the group of graduate students would depart for Buffalo in ten days because the dorms were closing down for the summer. Bill decided to call Christine again to tell her when he was leaving. She was upset and said that she wanted to see Bill one last time. She asked him if he could come to Hannover. Of course he agreed and the following morning he left Cologne to drive to Hannover. But things did not go well. His VW Beetle did not run smoothly. He pulled into a rest area along the Autobahn, where the motor just quit. He was trying to get it to run, when another VW pulled into the rest area. The driver tried to get the engine started but couldn't figure it out either. The driver asked Bill where he was going and, hearing Hannover, told Bill that he was going just past Hannover to Peine and could give him a ride.

Because he was leaving in a few days and because he did not know what to do with the car, Savery took the plates off the car and pushed the car over a bank into some trees at the rest area. Another VW Beetle! Three hours later he was dropped off in Hannover and he called Christine.

"I'm here," said Bill.

"You're late. I've been waiting for you."

"I had car problems; I had to abandon my car on the side of the Autobahn near Cologne. Can you come and meet me?"

"Where are you?"

"I'm at the Freizeitheim. Do you have your kids?" asked Bill.

"No, Juliane has taken them again to Schöningen but this time overnight.

An hour later they were finally together. Christine told Bill that her husband had gone to Munich for three days and that she wanted Bill to stay with her until noon the next day. She said she just wanted to relive the warmth and love and security that she had felt so often with him in Schöningen.

They started their last day together by renting a row boat as they had so many years before. Later they ate in a pleasant Turkish restaurant. Eventually they went to her apartment where they spent the evening and night in total but tearful happiness. Why did things always have to change?

A few days later Bill found himself sitting in a second-class, nonsmoking compartment in the Cologne-Frankfurt Airport express train, where he took part in friendly conversations with German passengers just as he had years before in the Frankfurt-Kassel express train and this time again he was mostly lost in thoughts of the past and the future: the past, where he had experienced his first true love, and the future, where new love was certainly waiting for him. For the first time in years peace and hope filled his heart.